ELEGANT PUNK

ALSO BY DARLIN' NEAL

Rattlesnakes & The Moon

Elegant
PUNK

Stories by

Darlin' Neal

Press 53
Winston-Salem

Press 53, LLC
PO Box 30314
Winston-Salem, NC 27130

First Edition

Cover art, "From Somewhere Else," Copyright © 2012
by Ashley Inguanta, used by permission of the artist.

Author photo by Sara Floyd.

Library of Congress Control Number: 2012901352

Printed on acid-free paper
ISBN 978-1-935708-50-6

For my mother and the beloved grandsons to whom she gave shelter,
Joseph Alexander Neal and James Robert Neal

For Brian and Sara

ACKNOWLEDGMENTS

The author gratefully acknowledges these fine publications where these stories first appeared:

"Misty Blue Waters" in *The Arkansas Review*
"Blue Star" in *Night Train*
"Weave," "A String of Catfish," and "Fumble" in *Freight Stories*
"Rust" and "Vitamins" in *The Lifted Brow*
"Stop" and "The Man From the Little Theater" in *Keyhole Magazine*
"Trace" and "Beret" in *Smokelong Quarterly*
"Pop," "Conservation," "Carriage," "Oil," and "Violin" in *elimae*
"Herald," in *Jabberwock Review*
"Polka Dot," in *Corium*
"Train" in *Eclectica Magazine*
"Zest" and "Sheets" in *Matter: The Journal of Compressed Literary Arts*
"Blue" in *The Los Angeles Review*
"Oysters" in *Kitty Snacks*
"The Sitter," in *Temenos*
"Legs" in *The Mississsippi Review*
"Honeymoon" in *Hobart*
"Powwow," "Four Hundred Miles," and "Woman" in *Wigleaf*
    ("Powwow" also appeared in *Best of The Web 2009*)
"Open House" in *The MacGuffin*
"Ramble" in *Juked*

Elegant Punk

Misty Blue Waters

At school she was Bitchy Boo Hoo. She was Slut Eyes. She was Fucking So Very Grave. Girls gawked and turned their backs and whispered and laughed when she passed. Kids said, "Your name is Redgrave, not Waters." They were so stupid. They didn't know anything. She was a freak and proud of it. Her daddy was a rock 'n' roll star. Her name was Misty Blue Waters and all that needed to be changed on the birth certificate was the last name, if she decided to make it legal. What the stupid asses didn't check were the CD covers with her dad's last name, Waters, on each and every single one. They lived in Memphis and they didn't know shit about music. *They* couldn't get in to a show just by saying their dad's last name. She didn't even have to say his name anymore, all she had to do was show up with her face. One day they would be a little older and they would *wish*.

She wouldn't have even gone to school that day but it was the deal she made with her mother, go and then you can spend the weekend with your dad. So she went and after school she took her time and got dressed for her date with Daddy and headed for The Young Avenue Deli. She couldn't stand to wait so many hours for the night to come in that house with no one to talk to. She was way too excited. At The Deli, everyone knew her. They said, Hey, Misty Blue, look at you! Look at your hair! Where'd you get that skirt? They loved the glitter on her eyes. She'd bleached her hair blonde with a tinge of pink dye on the ends. She found a poodle skirt at a vintage store. After all, he was taking her to meet a 50's retro band. She wore fishnet hose because to be a little sexy was important for a girl. She had been preparing for this weekend for two months. At least.

A stripper friend of her dad's, Crescent City Delilah, joined her at the bar.

CC Delilah said, "Misty Blue, you shouldn't be smoking." She shook her head and smiled.

Then she said, "What can I say, I started smoking at twelve. But I wish I hadn't. You'll wish you hadn't."

And, "What are you, all dressed up with nowhere to go?"

"Are you crazy?" Misty Blue said. "Dad's taking me to a show in Nashville. In a limousine."

CCD's face lit up with a smile and she adjusted Misty Blue's low-cut sweater a little. "Look at you growing up," she said. "And girl, you're going to be one of the lucky ones." Misty Blue knew what she meant and the compliment was a great one, coming from someone so endowed as CCD, and with all that great skin. CCD aimed her long fake lashes behind Misty Blue.

Wanda came in with a crooked, shiny walking stick and all that red hair and sat on the other side of her. She put her hand on Misty Blue's, who could have sworn the mood ring she wore turned from black to red at the touch.

"Hey, pretty girl," Wanda said. "I'm making ads for my restaurant. I want you to come and be in the photo shoot. Wear something wild." They talked about it for a while, but Misty Blue couldn't keep anything in, she was thinking about the night. The musicians would stare at her. Her dad would be so proud. She wrote the date of the shoot on her arm to remember.

She stared at Wanda dreaming. Wanda was old, but she was still so mysteriously beautiful. A lot of people thought Wanda had magic powers. Everyone talked to her with respect. She wore a black hat with a peacock feather in it. Behind Wanda, strips of shiny gold shimmered from ceiling to floor all across the empty stage.

The bartender brought Misty Blue a charred hamburger and a plate of spicy fries.

"God, I wish I could still eat like that," CCD said.

"Well, do then," Wanda said.

Misty Blue took a twenty out of her purse and offered it to the bartender. Wanda grabbed her wrist and reached inside her own silver purse. The bartender winked and shook his head at them both. She slid her near empty plate away. She jumped down from the barstool and kissed CCD and then Wanda. Wanda squeezed her inside all that warmth and all those wonderful scents and gave her a big smack on the cheek. Not until she was out of sight of the bar windows did she wipe the lipstick off.

At home she waited on the steps with the phone in her hand. She had on a gorgeous, white, fake-fur jacket. She had painted her shoes silver with bottles of nail polish.

She went in to check the time. She put her jacket on a hanger. She really didn't need it. She decided to have a beer, to pour it in a glass like a lady, but she knocked the glass off the counter and it shattered. She swept shards into a dustpan and took her beer outside. She waited for the limousine and she waited for a very long time, even though it didn't take long before she started saying to herself, "You knew better, stupid. This happens every time."

Last time, when her dad promised to make it up to her, he'd apologized and said he'd run in to some strippers. Who

3

could blame him? Strippers or a kid? Misty Blue blamed it on the drugs. She vowed to never do drugs.

In her mother's room was a long oval mirror. Misty Blue went in there and teased an imaginary audience. She wisped a scarf between her legs. She took her clothes off slowly, seeing the picture she made with each piece she removed, because this was art. She danced to no music. She wanted to keep listening for a limousine, just in case.

Stop

A young woman waits around a truck stop in a sundress. She imagines a stampede when the trucks fly past, honking, raising dust. When her uncle asked for the baby, she said, Okay. Okay, okay, okay, she says all the time. Oh, what she cannot hold. She cannot bear it. Even if she remains sitting, relief will come. She never even has to stand up, and no one will care. A rich, rich pretty woman, who sings for lots of money, buys that baby closet after closet full of clothes. She named the child Destiny. This moment remains always. There is no map out of here. Grease soaks the ground and she can't feel it when someone calls her a whore.

Trace

She thinks of birth, giving birth to herself, becoming another person, another dimension of a person. She taps dust with a fingertip. Her hand becomes a mystery of veins and light flickering from the edges.

She tells them she doesn't feel anything and then her head rests on the arm of the couch. Freddie Mercury sings, "Mama, just killed a man, put a gun against his head…," sounding so wonderful, filling the room. The singing and the story and the musicians all come in the room at once. She could touch them all. Bubba laughs, "You're taking off now."

"Why, Bubba?" she asks, meaning, why that name. A man so soft eyed and full lipped.

Her lover, she has not married him yet. She is seventeen. She lives with him in a little apartment that smells like metal and gasoline. He sits beside her watching the air. He is the only one who has ever been her lover.

On the wall hangs a shellacked photo of a guitar and flowers. Blankets cover the furniture. Through the doorway from the living room to the kitchen she sees the woman of the house standing in the open refrigerator. Bubba's wife. The woman of the house nibbles on a block of cheese like a rat.

The girl laughs. "Look! She's eating cheese!" The air from the refrigerator sweeps in and chills her. The woman of the house begins to cry. "Stop laughing at me."

"Hush," Bubba says. He has his hand on the girl's knee, moving her dress up a little higher on her thigh. She watches. "I'm cold," she says and Bubba rises to turn up the heat.

"What are you doing?" asks the woman of the house. She's come into the entrance now still holding the cheese.

"She's cold," Bubba says.

"Then throw her little ass out in the yard."

The girl laughs because she knows the woman should be jealous, has every right to be jealous, but rights don't make any sense. The dress cloth brushes tiny hairs against her thigh. Music grows and colorful birds sing in a giant cage. Everything is so beautiful with all the light trailing round.

Weave

The old truck was rusted. Its cab round. The whole thing full of soft edges, sitting in the weave of long, dried grass. No place for a key inside—a button someone pushed long ago, before they went somewhere over the grass then fresh with cows ambling through and gnawing it close. A boy kissed a girl on the new leather. Someone called him a punk though no one knew then about the punks we are now— how that word came to mean toughness turned to mutilation, for some, then commodified and back 'round again. The toll we pay to feel anything, for feeling too much.

Back then there was just a boy kissing a girl who would leave him one day because he was poor and she more educated and these things come to matter more than kisses and getting lost in touch. As unbelievable as that can be. A boy who went out to that field and stole a watermelon that rode in the back of the truck with them, waiting for later, while they watched East of Eden at a drive-in.

They beat him that night, for being with her, for what he stole that she gave. For what they suspected. He'd dropped her off and walked her to the door of her beautiful house. He got away from the beating like a fast sly animal and hid beneath bushes, not breathing, branches breaking around him, until they were gone. Bleeding, he made it through that night and married her anyway and they had a child, a brother I never met.

A String of Catfish

When I saw the dough I thought she was making pancakes, but it was too white and I realized, biscuits, of course, not even homemade anymore but from a can she'd popped open. I remembered the blackberries in the freezer. I cooked them with sugar. We ate and she told stories suspicious about why I'd come back after so many years, but it was just for those stories, to hear how I'd come flying out of the chicken coop backwards after sneaking inside, trying to fetch an egg, to remember the taste of fresh milk, a kitten catching milk from a stream in the air, to see the place I lived when I was first born, the house with those lace curtains, the woods where my father played and all my life had told me stories about. His brother threw a pitchfork and caught him in the thigh. I remembered the sting of piss ants clinging to my toes. I used a poker in the fireplace to make the warmth brighter. I loved the flying ashes. I held my daughter a little and rocked even though she was really too big to hold like that. My uncle came to the house and I was looking through a box of pictures. As a child I looked so tough holding a string of catfish above my head, standing on a chair while that string reached to the floor. I asked but he wouldn't let me take them and make copies. Maybe he'd figure something out. He didn't want to lose the pictures. I helped him rake the leaves and he spoke in Bible verses and reminded me that so had my grandfather. I told him I didn't know if I could live in Mississippi again but I was missing home, and he told me, no, that the way I thought, a white girl who would march for MLK, who didn't believe in a gender for God, it wouldn't be the whites that would kill me but the blacks. I was remembering being…

I was remembering being four beside a pond, not knowing the difference between me and the little black boy who waved from the other side, my uncle teaching me how to hook a worm and toss the line out just so. I was watching my grandmother listen to the magnolia leaves and blossoms in the wind. I was realizing all the ways I'd never look my uncle in the eyes again.

Fumble

She was thinking of beauty, sitting out there on her steps with the stars illuminating the desert world silver all the way to the mountains. Yucca, mesquite, rocks and barbed-wired fences sparkled beneath that light. If you stared, you could see inside the shadows. Her son, head hung beneath that blue cap and cigarette dangling, had gone home crying. She'd sent him, promised: tomorrow I'll start calling doctors. He'd come over with her granddaughter who'd left before he did, one home close enough to another to walk. The child had been dressed as a lamb, with grand coal eyelashes and a tail with a fuzzy end, for a play at school. She, the grandmother, hadn't been invited. Watching the child leave she'd thought of sheep in The Bible, how some believed blind following was the way to God. The world was heaven—that's what her own mother had believed. On earth we get our heaven. On earth we get our hell.

On TV someone was yelling about a fumble. Usually she cared, but the dark of the house was nice, the remote next to her hand. She pushed the button and it was so quiet she could hear telephone wires buzzing from pole to pole, carrying messages.

She thought of calling her children. One son's wife had

a beeper she didn't need. A little grown dog who fit in a teacup and used the litter box like a cat.

The son who'd left crying was her oldest, a man who drank too much but worked hard and was successful. Everyone had been worried about his liver for a long time. Out there in the desert she remembered his horrified face when she'd asked him to touch her. "Feel," she had said, guiding his hand to the soft cotton of her blouse, beneath to her breast. The horror had deepened with what followed. You haven't told Dad? Bigger than a golf ball, not as big as an orange. Flicking ashes out into the desert, he'd recited references that meant nothing, really, to either of them. She knew important measurements would be discussed in terms of stages. Stages used to be such innocent things, steps taken, needs no longer needs.

She closed her eyes against the memory of his crying and opened them to the starlight turning the desert to a heaven of light and shapes.

Beret

Len's five-year-old brother sat at the table wearing Stephen's beret. It looked ridiculous, covering that little scalp like a way-too-big shower cap that kept falling over his eyes. Stephen had worn that cap on a first date. He'd been allowed to drive the seventy miles to Las Cruces to the theater with a girl, because he was the oldest, and because he was their mother's favorite.

"It chaps my ass," Len had told him. "All the crap she lets you get away with." Stephen had doubled over laughing so hard about Len's chapped ass that Len couldn't help but laugh too.

And then, Stephen, who read all the time and dreamed of acting, said, "Don't speak in clichés."

That was six months ago.

Now, Len pointed a fork at the ridiculous five-year-old in the beret and said, "Shut up, Tommy. I mean it."

Mother said, "My brother Don threw a fork at me when we were kids. It got stuck right here." She pointed to the crease below her brow bone. "When I blinked, it moved and cracked us up."

"How did you get it out?" Tommy asked.

"Don jerked it free."

"Lucky you're not blind."

"Lucky I'm not a lot of things."

"What did your mother do?"

"Nothing that I remember. I think we carried on with dinner."

"He does have too much syrup."

"I told you to shut up about my food."

"Syrup butt," Tommy said.

Mother said, "Navajos don't have such a word in their vocabulary, you know that? It's like telling someone not to breathe, to die, because words are breath."

"Like I said, 'shut up!'" Len said, and then he felt sort of sick, but when Mother said, "Don't do that, Len," he said, "You couldn't blame me if he died. That's hocus pocus."

"Not saying shut up is manners is what it is, and kindness. Just eat your pancakes and be quiet."

"So what's the difference?"

"The difference?"

"In be quiet and shut up?"

"It's politer."

"You're still telling me don't breathe, right?"

He wanted her to get mad, but, calmly, she said, "Eat your pancakes. Have all the syrup you want."

And then she was listening to Tommy, who pushed the beret from his eyes and said: "Will you make me something like a crepe? With cheese inside?"

Mother carried batter to the stove and forgot what she was doing. She went to the sink and started washing dishes. She stared through the window. Outside motorcycles roared through the desert. Len knew what she imagined—the ditch in the distance where the power line had dropped that broke Stephen's neck and stopped his breath forever.

Upstairs Boy

Carter stood, sweating in the damn heat, on the basketball court outside The Youth Crisis Center with seven other boys, while Dr. C preached about the evils of masturbation. Eight of them lined up against the wall as she ordered the evening counselor to frisk them for cigarettes. She smelled nicotine everywhere.

She marched away. Carter could see her through the side entrance taking out her key and unlocking the desk drawer to gather belongings. "Bitch," he whispered, imagining his mother right there, nodding in approval.

The evening counselor smoked himself and he didn't put much into the searching. He was an all right guy, even if he was a little too happy and looked like a hippie.

"I will find them," Dr. C said, coming back out with a big ugly white purse. "And there will be consequences."

Then she dismissed them to play basketball so they could go kill one another. Carter and Dustin, the smallest, stayed on the sidewalk. There were four other downstairs guys, Simon, Sam, Roscoe and Harvard, out there playing, too. All the upstairs kids, except Carter and Dustin, had been removed from the Center last week when some old kid got caught upstairs with his pants down, holding a little guy to his crotch and beating the kid over the head with a book he was supposed to be downstairs reading. A night watchman had called the cops. Human Services removed the youngest kids and the caught molester. Dr. C. fired the night watchman. She acted mad at Cheeseburger who had sent the watchman to check upstairs.

"I wonder how much they pay that crazy bitch," Carter said, as she slid into a gas-guzzling Lincoln parked under an oak in the lot.

"Who?" Dustin asked in his muffled voice, his hearing aid about gone useless. He had been learning sign language. Carter studied with him, as if in a million years they'd keep knowing each other.

"Dr. C," Carter replied.

"Yeah," Dustin said. "I'd like to kill that crazy bitch and drain her pockets."

"Kill her?" Carter pushed Dustin off the sidewalk into the dirt. "You don't want to kill her, asshole."

"Sure, I do," he said, ducking as tall Cheeseburger came flying over, spun around and away like some miracle, and sunk the ball into the basket before cracking an elbow down into Kyle's eye socket. The shiner would be beautiful and that fucking molester Kyle deserved it. He never got caught doing anything.

As Kyle screamed, Carter watched a blue jay fly above and land on the balcony by the room where the Upstairs Boys, he and Dustin, and all boys fourteen and under, slept.

Carter remembered his mother's brother who used to watch out for him, like Cheeseburger did now, sitting at a kitchen table in a little trailer with his hands shaking, talking about molesters bragging in jail. He remembered the curl of those strong hands and fingers wishing for a neck to break. If Carter's uncle were around, he'd kill Kyle. If his mother were here, they'd all be buddies with Cheeseburger.

Both were in prison, his uncle for he didn't know how long, his mother for one more year.

She was due out in the next summer. She'd be standing in that doorway waiting with a Big Gulp. He hoped she'd think he'd grown enough in five years. "Come on, bud," she'd say. "Let's get you away from here." Then she'd look at Dr. C. "You crazy bitch. You don't know a thing about sex, or Jesus."

God, he missed her. Wishing for hurried time made the whole world feel listless. It made him want to fall to sleep. She must not be able to afford stamps, or her letters had been lost or stolen lately, now that he'd moved around too many places. They were best friends. She didn't like to be anywhere without him. Until his grandma died two years ago, the old woman had taken him to see his mother once a week in prison. It was a long drive through the desert. They'd take sandwiches to eat along the way and listen to the radio when it got reception. They'd take a break in the ride and eat a buffet lunch at an Indian Casino. They'd drive farther and farther into the middle of nowhere until Carter saw the building that looked like a school with razor wire on top of a chain link fence. His grandmother would leave her purse in the car. He'd make sure his pockets were empty before he got out. They'd wait for a buzzer and enter a cement-walled hallway, the chain link and razor wire extending above his head, and then through another door. His grandma would leave her license at a hole in a window where the woman behind it was sometimes nice and sometimes a bitch. They'd get x-rayed. His grandmother would bring change and they'd all have Cokes and candy bars and chips sitting in chairs across little tables from each other, their own little area. They ignored the other prisoners talking with friends and family. They weren't allowed to hug or touch, but his mother blew kisses he could feel on his eyelashes. It was so much better than jail where you talked on a phone and looked at each other through glass. He'd sit there not caring as much as his grandma did that she'd shaved off her long hair. They'd stay for every minute of their two hours and then they'd be waving goodbye. He'd walk back out past the x-ray machine, the window where they got their stuff again, back through the cement hall with that chain link at the top, out into all that sky and desert. He thought he could hear it. His mother going back inside, through door after door, until she came to a cage and got shut inside. She went through so many cages to get to the one where she lived. Cages inside cages. He could picture her room, almost as small as the cement hall he left through, two small beds against each wall, a toilet, a TV. His grandmother had given her the TV. His mother would go sit in there and write him a letter. He'd heard people talking. He wished the guards wouldn't bring her any more drugs. His grandma hoped and hoped they'd all have a new start.

Then his grandma died and he got sent to relatives in Mississippi where all the trees closed in on him, and the humidity made his clothes sticky and heavy. He felt homesick. He didn't like living with strangers any more than his mother did. She sent letters all the time talking about how much she wanted out, how she would do right this time. He was tired of waiting. He threw too many fits and the great aunt at the house he was sent to decided she couldn't handle him. Her husband was a man who always wore plaid. He'd taken Carter in his truck to another brick building, walked him inside and said to a woman, "Here he is." And then to Carter, "Sorry, boy." That was when Carter started the rounds of foster homes and getting into trouble, for throwing rocks and breaking windows of an abandoned house, for stealing a newlywed couple's wedding presents out of their fancy trailer. Great gifts he would have given one day to his mother. The big sister of the boy he stole with told on them. Carter almost made himself believe all those riches they carried away in sheets might have been abandoned: vases from the living room tables, silverware still in boxes from the kitchen cabinets, jewelry from inside the tiny drawers on top of the bedroom dresser.

No more foster homes agreed to take him since he'd shoved that carrot down that bully's throat at the last house and almost choked the bastard to death.

Don't end up in trouble like me, his mother had written. *When I get out, we'll buy a trailer and move to Ruidoso where the cops won't even know I've ever been in trouble. I know somebody in here who knows one I can afford. We'll get a big screen TV. We'll fence the yard if it isn't already so you can have a dog.*

For three months now he hadn't had a letter. He'd been asking everyone he saw to please make sure she knew this last address. She hadn't been able to keep up with where he was. He lived in The Youth Crisis Center, a yellow, three-story building next door to an abandoned gas station. The boys staying at the Center awaited placement or some magical time like the summer in that distant year. Kyle had been kicked out of detention, Dustin dismissed from the state mental hospital. The rest were heading for those very places or, like Carter, hoping for a new foster home. Someone somewhere was supposed to be making decisions about the future of each.

Carter tried to keep focused. He kept thinking: don't steal, make good grades, don't get mad. You want to be with your mama next summer, not in permanent detention or off tried as an adult. His pocket wallet held photos but no money to catch a bus ride. There was a photo of his pretty mama with those tattooed arms: a pussycat hugging an old-timey whiskey bottle, a hand spanning her forearm.

Someone must have needled that when she was high. There was a photo of an old bulldog named Bruno who'd gotten taken away from his grandma's house when Carter did. He hoped wrinkly-faced Bruno was still alive. When he lived with his mama, he'd find another bulldog. He thought about the contents of his pocket, and the important thing: nothing was stolen. He worked hard on not stealing. That was the number-one goal on his behavior plan, the plan that would help free him come next summer.

He and Dustin crouched by the chain-link fence, throwing rocks into a paper cup that had flown over with some other trash. Carter got three in a row, so he won.

Dustin stood unfisting a spray of gravel. He wiped his palms on his pants. He looked toward the court nodding and dreaming. He reminded Carter of a beat dog, the way his eyes never focused and he shifted weight from leg to leg. Out of the blue, he laughed his terrible sounding laugh, like a Muppet, like Froggy or Ernie or something. And he was twelve. Then he screamed, "Cover me, Cheeseburger!" and ran as fast as he could and rammed his big round head into Kyle's ribs. The boys piled into a tangle of legs and bodies. Carter shook his head as the night counselor called, "Hey! Hey!" He didn't understand his buddies, Dustin or Cheeseburger, why the behavior plan meant nothing to them. The guys just didn't connect points and privileges.

Everyone untangled fine and lined up at the door, except Dustin who dug at his ear and then started crawling around searching for his hearing aid, and Cheeseburger who helped him look. Finally Cheeseburger found it and the two joined Carter, who motioned like a gentleman and said, "You guys first." He didn't like people to walk behind him. Tonight had been a regular after-dinner game except there was no blood. *Crazy bastards*, Carter thought following them in. *Murderous motherfuckers*. They took turns washing up, without watching one another and causing more trouble, then dispersed into the living room to view the movie Dr. C had rented: *The Lion King*. All they got to watch was fucking kid movies and *Sesame Street*, and, Carter, the youngest, was eleven years old!

Carter wondered how long this latest evening counselor would last. He'd already had broken ribs and a nasty bite, but that was from a couple of the kids who'd been sent off. He did things like make extra tea and bring in treats some evenings. Tonight he brought lemons and sugar and let Dustin and Carter help make a batch. They were the only two interested in helping. Everyone got a glass and a piece of banana bread the guy's hippie girlfriend had made.

While they were slicing the bread into nine equal pieces with a plastic knife, Carter noticed the tiny hole in the hippie's ear. "Dr. C make you take your earring out?" he asked.

The counselor shrugged.

"You think that's her right?" Cheeseburger asked.

The evening counselor smiled. "Go on into the TV room. Just don't make a mess." He stepped out on the balcony, where he could watch them and smoke at once, there by the punching bag.

Past the window, down below, Carter saw a Sheriff's car patrolling the Center parking lot, and farther down past the gas station a road that led into town, where people roamed, having fun and getting into trouble. The counselor was gazing that way, wanting to be with that banana-bread-making woman somewhere, you could bet on it.

The sun beat straight through the balcony doors. Carter was so hot. He gulped his lemonade and stared at his empty glass. He was hot and he didn't want to ask for what he should be able to just get up and pour.

Dustin lay on the rug concentrating on TV, wishing he could read their lips. That was something he could do with people, but not animated characters. He'd left his lemonade on the table between Cheeseburger and Carter. Carter took the full glass and replaced it with his empty one, drinking this time with shaky hands.

When Dustin reached for his lemonade, Carter got calm. Dustin rose up in front of him.

Carter shrugged, putting on the innocence.

"Move out the damn view," Cheeseburger said, toeing Dustin away so he could watch the movie.

"All you fuck ups!" Dustin screamed. He clawed at his own face. "You sick fuck ups!"

"What's going on?" the evening counselor called and Dustin ran to the balcony and announced: "I'm going to kill myself!"

An audience gathered in the exhaust-filled air.

"Over a damn glass of lemonade?" Cheeseburger asked.

"Let's see you," said Kyle.

The counselor asked again, "What's going on?"

"Someone drank his lemonade," said Carter, making sure not to say, "Stole," with his lips that tasted of lemon and sugar and ice.

"I'll make you another," the counselor said.

"Who drank it?" Dustin yelled.

"Have the rest of mine," said Carter, offering a half empty glass. "I don't like the sour shit anyway."

"There wasn't a big limit," the counselor said. "You don't have to think that way."

Dustin glared, then punched not Carter, but Cheeseburger in the leg.

"Ow, bitch!" Cheeseburger said.

Carter threw the lemonade in Dustin's face. Dustin responded by running straight toward and over the ledge.

The counselor dove in the direction the little guy had gone, his cigarette flying, and ash sparkling. Everyone quieted, listening for the thud, until, somehow, the counselor came up with a handful of jeans that had Dustin attached. Cheeseburger got there and helped pull the kid back to safety, saying, "Dumb assed little cracker."

Carter stood, holding the empty glass and feeling exposed.

In bed that night, Carter could hear Dustin crying soft. He wondered what the guy worried over. It never turned good to ask someone about where they'd been. You never got the truth. He kept thinking what he'd thought, for that split second when his friend went over the edge, I wonder what he'll look like smashed. He was grateful his friend didn't die or splinter. He wished he hadn't stolen. He wanted to be the kind of guy who fixed things instead. A stand-up friend, like Cheeseburger. The evening counselor had talked to Dustin for a while, got him to punch his anger out. He'd let Carter hold the bag and punch with him, as if he knew, until the rest of them finished the movie. The evening counselor had squeezed another batch of lemonade and let them drink until their stomachs ached.

Carter heard what sounded like mice in the walls.

"Hey," he whispered. "Hey, Dustin? You know as long as Cheeseburger's here? Kyle ain't going to turn up here."

But Dustin was already asleep.

The next morning was a Saturday and they rode in a van to a church. Dr. C was in the front passenger seat, smiling. Carter was trying to look at her and figure out who she really was. She'd pulled him aside before they left and told him, "I found your mother at the prison in Grants, New Mexico. I called and made them give me her address." Then she'd handed him a piece of paper with all that information he would have had memorized if his grandma hadn't been the one to address the envelopes: his mother's state prisoner number, her cell block, the address for the prison. He imagined the warning on the letters that would come his way when he started getting letters again, *you are receiving this from an inmate...*

Dr. C had sacrificed her weekend to accompany them on the field trip. She didn't often smile. She'd said she'd worked hard to get them seats at this church service, in this part of town. She said the purpose of this particular experience was to show them where they might live and work one day if they tried hard and maybe even got themselves into college. She had white hair that reminded Carter of curlers. The jackets of her suit dresses looked as if they were cutting her in two. He didn't know why she didn't just unbutton. He remembered the swing of his mama's hips when she walked in heels, the spill of her breasts. Days at the center, Dr. C's high heels lay beneath the desk. She pretty much stayed glued to the seat of her chair. You'd stand before her and receive your medicine, reprimands, and praise. All of which she recorded in a notebook for the decision makers. Now she'd confused him by giving him what he wanted more than anything else.

The van sped along Fortification Street. *Fornication Street* all the boys were thinking. *Fornication Street.*

The van exited to 55. Everything was green. Carter looked through trees to the sky, loving the motion of going somewhere and the dangerous feeling of sharp curves. There wasn't a cloud in the sky, but he thought he could smell rain.

Dustin whispered, "Pardon me. Pardon me. Pardon me, sir." He liked to repeat words, over and over. It bugged the crap out of Carter. If you hushed him, he'd get right up in your face and repeat and repeat fast as he could. Instead, Carter tried distraction.

"I used to live off that exit."

"So," Dustin said. "Where?"

"I'm not sure," Carter said. "Some house. I think the street was Briarwood." He remembered coats piled in a corner of a dark room. A dog tied to a tree. The streets had grown icy and the lights had gone out. He'd brushed the dog beside a gas heater when they finally let it come inside. A huge dog that stunk. The black fur had golden shades in it that matched the colors of the flames. The dog licked his face clean. He didn't remember the people there. Just the dog.

They rode down Lakeland Boulevard and off into the parking lot of one of the biggest churches Carter had seen with the highest roof and massive colorful windows. The van went silent.

Dr. C opened the doors and led the way. Inside everywhere Carter looked some rich white dude was gawking at him. Carter was white too but he'd never worn a suit that he could remember and he didn't like the way these guys stared.

He did not want to shake the bastards' hands, but there were smiles you gave, things you did to get by. He kept his goals in mind. Upon his mother's release next summer, he'd have a clean record, and they'd find a home.

Looking toward the pulpit, he felt tiny as nothing. Everything was shine and polish. Carter thought he'd walked into a palace of riches. Jewels everywhere. Expensive glass. A church for rich people. Packed full.

All the Crisis Center guys fidgeted, except Kyle who gave girls his sleepy stare and got pity for that black eye. It occurred to Carter that Kyle was the most successful of them all. Everywhere they went the guy made friends. Carter really hated the sneaky bastard. He was tall and thin and had dark razor stubble. He had a bad-boy saunter. His upper lip went crooked when he smiled to make the girls swoon. He winked at one and happy giggles rippled from her through a group of girls and echoed beneath the ceiling.

Dr. C took them to the second row and lined them up disastrously: Cheeseburger, Kyle, Dustin, and Carter, with the other four guys, Simon, Sam, Harvard and Roscoe in the row behind.

The first speaker walked by carrying a briefcase in one hand and an armload of papers she'd managed not to drop when she tripped over a bump in the rug.

Kyle leaned forward so she could see him better. "Need help with those things?"

Her long hair was the color of dark mud. She had the sides pulled back in silver barrettes so tightly the torque slanted her small eyes. Carter wondered if she liked to play at being a little girl to turn guys on. She was thin lipped and wore large glasses. She must have been at least thirty. Even so, Carter thought she might have been pretty, but her eyes were also the color of mud and the blankest and meanest he'd seen. Even when she smiled and said to Kyle, "No thank you. I can manage," her eyes didn't light a flicker. But she was female. She smelled expensive and she wore a snug skirt so you could see the outline of her butt and thighs.

As she walked away, Cheeseburger whispered, "Baby's got more cakes than Duncan Hines."

Dr. C cleared her throat disapprovingly.

At the podium, the speaker welcomed the special guests from the Youth Crisis Center. All the Crisis Center guys looked down.

The speaker talked about how years ago she'd committed a horrible sin. She'd murdered her baby.

"Oh, my," whispered Dr. C.

"Is this really what they gonna preach about tonight?" Cheeseburger asked.

"Just hush," Dr. C whispered. "I'm sure it's not a one-topic service. Pay attention to where you are."

"Abortion is ungodly," said the speaker. "Feminists are trying to take women away from the role God intended."

Kyle looked down and snickered. He grabbed his crotch.

"I ain't planning an abortion, are you?" Cheeseburger said and they all laughed. Carter could swear when Dr. C tilted her head in warning that there was a little smile trying to come out the corner of her lips.

Dustin touched Kyle's arm, trying to look over at Cheeseburger, and got pushed away. Carter knew Dustin wanted to ask what was so annoying and funny.

The woman used those words, the unborn, which sounded strange to Carter. Unborn, undead, he thought. She turned on a Power Point projector. She clicked through pictures. She pointed out nubs and fingers and toes from three weeks to nine months of the unborn babies all jammed up inside those wombs.

Carter couldn't for the life of him figure those slides of babies in trashcans. First why they were showing them to a bunch a guys, and second, none of the babies looked unborn. They were bigger than the nine-month slide and looked like clean dolls. He'd heard babies were born bloody. A girl had one in a bathroom stall at school and a girl who saw said it was a mess.

Kyle grabbed Dustin's hand and Dustin made a choking sound. Seeing Kyle squeeze Dustin's hand was like seeing someone strangled and Carter started to yell but Cheeseburger already had Kyle by the throat.

"Let go," Cheeseburger said, eyes fluttering like a blind man. "Now."

The speaker stopped talking about the unborn and said, "Jesus help us."

Dr. C smiled at her to continue and she did, talking now

about the importance of family values as Kyle let go of Dustin and Cheeseburger let go of Kyle. She went on and on about the purpose of women, the importance of mothers. Carter remembered his beautiful mother, so tender. The speaker had a group picture—grandparents, parents and children all together. Sometimes Carter missed his grandfather, missed living with his grandma, but that was like missing being a kid. Sometimes he thought he'd call up one of the search programs on TV and have them look for his father. He didn't know if his father was alive. He was resolved he'd never know who the guy was until everyone's DNA became searchable and registered on computers. He supposed it didn't matter.

Dustin wept.

Kyle clutched at his own throat.

Dr. C pointed at Cheeseburger threateningly and started writing in her notebook.

There was a pop of Dustin slapping Kyle to get his attention. He was showing Kyle his fingers. Carter was shocked to see all the scratches from where Kyle had dug his nails in. Kyle made to grab Dustin's hand again, but the kid moved quick, wiping his snotty nose on Kyle's arm. When Kyle caught Dustin's hand a second time, Carter dove over his friend and started punching. The echoes of the curses, kicked wood and cries rippled along the church ceiling. Cheeseburger got the guy by the neck again and Carter kept on punching.

"That was a sad show," Dustin said from his bed that night.

Carter shrugged. What they were really thinking they didn't want to talk about, how the police had come and taken Cheeseburger back to detention.

Kyle had gut-punched Carter on the way to the van and his stomach was sore. He moved into light so Dustin could see his lips when he spoke. "It was a bunch of shit," he said.

The show had gone on, even without Cheeseburger. The final video depicted kids in Africa so starved they looked like ancient, ancient skeletal people. "We should all thank God we live in America," the speaker had said.

"I don't like that church," Dustin amended.

"Some of it was true," Carter said. It worried at him that Dr. C had sent only Cheeseburger away. Why not him? "Some of it was sad."

A new speaker had talked about drugs and temporary depraved fun, finally showing a video of a man shaking with what was called Parkinson's disease. That was what Ecstasy would do for you.

"Think they'll send Cheeseburger back here?" Dustin asked.

"Quiet in there," the evening counselor called, walking back down the stairs and away. He'd go home and the guards would be down there, indifferent to anything but keeping them all inside.

A street light died outside and Carter watched the darkness rise to the ceiling. He wondered what stabbing someone felt like. He imagined stabbing Kyle. He wondered if he could do it. He closed his eyes against the thick black. The air felt stale. It was quiet. Any whispering sounded far away. He imagined gates closing, in detention, in prison. He wished he could put Kyle in a dark hole somewhere with a metal door he'd never open. He wished someone would listen to them about Cheeseburger, that they could break him out.

He sat back up. "Let's go someplace they won't find us," he said.

Dustin looked confused so Carter stood, stuffed blankets around pillows like some silly fool from TV. He offered his hand.

"What?" Dustin asked. "Crazy," he said, reaching and smiling.

Carter walked with him to a closet down the hallway and opened the door. "Get in," he said.

Dustin's eyes grew big and his laugh nervous. So Carter squeezed in first and sat down, patting the floor next to him. Dustin sat, trembling.

"Keep quiet," Carter said.

He tested the knob, that he'd be able to open it from the inside. He closed the door. He put his arm around his buddy. He rested his cheek on Dustin's stubbly hair. "I can sleep sitting up. Can you?" Dustin reached up and touched his cheek, trying to understand. His hand dropped. Carter listened to the floor, to the sound in the walls, to the noise coming from the street. In a while he realized he'd kissed Dustin's big funny head and that Dustin was asleep. That easy, like a baby.

He heard thunder blasting outside and listened for footsteps creeping, for the sound of sheets moving. He heard more far-away whispering.

He thought of Pennsylvania. He remembered it as green and dark with rain washing down a windshield. That's where he lived with his mother until she gave up and moved back to New Mexico. The last time he saw her, he was only six years old. She had the longest golden hair. It really was golden. She was thin. She wore a short skirt, a tight T-shirt. A man stood in a doorway and waved from beneath an umbrella. The man winked at Carter. "Duck down," his mother whispered, driving around a corner, away from the man. She stopped and stepped out.

"Come on, Carter," she said soft as a nighttime prayer. The keys in her hand jingled. She opened the trunk. Carter had a blanket and a pillow in there. His mother's nails were long and the blackest red. "Hop in," she said. "For just a bit."

He got in and she closed the lid. The car moved awhile and stopped. He could hear the door open and close. A man's voice. He liked it when they stayed inside the car and he knew he wasn't by himself.

He'd wait for the rocking, for the moans to rise and fall and finish. In a while she'd open the lid. Sometimes she'd take him for a burger or an ice cream. She'd wipe his face clean with Baby Wipes. She always had Baby Wipes in the car.

Rust

Even in the dark restaurant he could see some strange speck of something like light in the girl's eye. In a booth, she sat with a man who must have been her father with a tattoo of a skunk on his upper arm. Underneath it read: Stinky. The little girl whose hair fizzed like electric cotton, sang to this man, "I see the moon, the moon sees me, I hope that moon don't tell on me."

"I refute that," someone from another booth said, sounding wrong and strange like someone who belonged in college or court.

Plants grew like scraggly weeds here in neon containers with paint on the walls the color of the sky and sea and grass. A place so far from home. He could never go home now. He waited for someone to smile at him. The man with the tattoo helped the child slide from her seat. She waddled away.

He thought of a man, a father he'd known, a friend since childhood, in a car somewhere looking for more meth. The guy was talking about not going home. There were three of them sitting in a truck outside a dark rusty trailer park in the desert and the guy was smiling, talking about not going home. He remembered how he'd noticed the stars that were always there and that moon so large and far away and how the guy kept talking and the knife in his hand that didn't make sense and how the guy started stabbing the man in the middle, his brother who had a bloody arm raised and blood welling on his knee and all over his jeans.

He'd gotten out and ran to the passenger side with a bat from the truck bed. His strength surprised him and left an indentation in the man's skull. The man kept standing there with that knife so he kept slamming him with that bat.

When the man finally fell, just in the short distance was a white diaper and hair with barrettes that caught that moonlight, a sudden child waddling down the gravel road into the rust and the darkness.

Vitamins

The preacher came by early that morning to find out why they hadn't been in church. Mom and Dad were at the horse races. He'd asked why it was so hot in the house, fanning himself, and it was only then the girl realized how uncomfortable it was inside. He found the thermostat and turned down the heater she'd turned up too high, shaking his head but he didn't say anything else except, "Tell your parents I came by."

She took the children outside, a baby, a toddler, and a little brother. Her sandal broke. The strap flapped around so much she took her shoes off and walked on the dusty ground with a toddler on one hip. She didn't wear shoes much outside anyway when she was playing and her feet were tough against anything but the goats' heads.

The little boy kept slapping two sticks gently that had leaves on the end that floated together and released. It made her think of forceps, of a baby she'd seen recently who had his head smashed in above his ears. She wondered if he'd grow up to look like a cone head. She was bored taking care of babies. She was ten.

There was instant pudding in the cabinet. There were vitamins. Her mother would cook when she got home that

35

night, or if they won money, maybe they'd bring something. The girl didn't feel like making pudding. She asked her brother did he want to take a bunch of vitamins and see what happened? Maybe they would become incredibly strong. He didn't, but she did.

When she got sick that night her vomit was the brightest deepest yellow. She didn't die like she felt like she would, vomiting and vomiting, but it was a sign of things to come.

Pop

Outside a golden horse with the longest mane pranced 'round. A man gave her an orange drink. He said, "Pop," like no one around here. She kept thinking of the sound the can made opening.

She'd never seen the man before. Her stepfather sent her outside to watch the horses. As if she didn't know what the little vial on the table held or hadn't heard the bubbling inside a bong by now.

In the man's arms, being carried farther from the house, she imagined the horse wore a saddle. She could feel herself separate from those hands, made out of air, as she ran and jumped on, riding in circles, waiting somewhere else.

Herald

Angelina sat on a brick fence watching the clouds of her breath. In the distance, she could hear Jose blaring on his trumpet. He played loud and outside early in the morning to wake and irritate people. "Pay back for my misery," he'd say. His mother and father were both gone to work by 6:00 and he had to be dressed from top to bottom, hair slicked smooth and socks folded and warm inside his shoes. He'd bragged to Angelina about being chased down an alleyway by a woman with a frying pan. He'd bragged about a fevered old lady who couldn't speak or get up but pleaded with her eyes for him to go away from her window. When that old lady died, he'd told Angelina, "Guess I heralded her in."

From where she sat, she could see two rooms inside Marianna's house—the kitchen with its black and white tiles that shone like marble. Tiny red chilies dotted the wallpaper. On the dividing wall between the kitchen and the den was a chili ristra. There the floor turned hardwood and on the far wall stood a fireplace with the cat Angelina herself had sculpted. It was white with emerald eyes and paws ready to pounce. In the corner was Marianna's cello which she practiced everyday and which allowed her frequently to wear sequined dresses and head into Houston to play solo on a stage.

Marianna came into the room in a red robe and ignited a newspaper in the fireplace. Flames puffed up and down behind her as she drew near the window in front of Angelina. She slid it open just enough to talk.

"Come over after school. I'm going to make homemade pita bread for my dinner date tomorrow." Marianna was always coming over to the house where Angelina lived with Aunt Carmela. She was always talking about her broken heart or disappointment. She didn't want to have babies with men with poor manual dexterity or who were bad at math. She didn't want to pass such things on to her children. Still, some guy was always coming over. "I'll teach you how to make a Greek feast before you move away."

Angelina was leaving Texas to move back in with her father in New Mexico. She didn't want to leave and be so far away from a woman's guidance. After all that's why her father said he sent her.

"We've got three weeks. We could try a dozen different ethnicities," said Marianna.

"I'll be here," Angelina said, jumping down from the fence.

Marianna said, "Here comes that little bastard."

Jose was coming down the alleyway, trumpet in its case, books in his backpack.

As Angelina and Jose walked away, Marianna called, "Four o'clock," and slid the window closed.

Jose's cheeks were terribly red from the cold and from blowing on the trumpet. He smelled like some awful old man's after shave. He'd been wanting to kiss Angelina and she thought that he'd be a good start.

Polka Dot

Maybe I wore a polka dot dress when I slid over the seat. If my panties showed, I wouldn't have thought much about it, just pulled my dress down when I got to the front, wanting the radio but we couldn't run down the battery. The parking lot was crowded with empty cars over gravel. We could see mountains bluish all around. I could hear the announcer in the distance, people cheering on the track. A man walked by carrying a folding chair. He had afro curly hair; he was white. He seemed sort of like a rich man to me, from somewhere else when he leaned to the window and asked me how old I was. I told him. Was it 11? My brother locked the back doors and fell over the seat beside me to lock the front and he breathed so scared as the man walked back by the car. "Don't look, don't look," he said as the man walked by and I glimpsed at the man playing with himself as he slowed down, probably thinking he was crafty, hiding his limp dick from everyone else with that folding chair. It was hot in the treeless parking lot. All I gave him was my profile.

Blue Star

Maggie is nineteen. Her muscles and joints ache. She feels like she has the flu, and old. She lives on Baltimore Street with a stripper named Susan. Susan's acting crazy, giggling and jabbering away in the high voice of a child, then crying about a lost boyfriend.

"Shut up!" Maggie says. "I don't know what's worse—when you giggle or when you cry."

Maggie is a little girl. All the kids in her evening day care make up stories. The teacher holds a notebook and writes them down. Maggie's are filled with details and movement: One day a man and a woman were walking through the desert and, Poof! They were gone...A skunk and a jackrabbit went to Hobbs...They dined on Granddaddy's chili and cheese...Oh skunk! Oh skunk! You elegant punk. With you I'd like to roam....

She tells her teacher she has no bed in her home. She tells her teacher she's always in the corner. She says, I'm the little girl that no one loved.

Oh dear, says Mrs. Bailey. Maggie, you have to know that's not true.

It is, says Maggie. Then she whispers, but don't tell anyone.

Mrs. Bailey wishes Maggie would act her age and she says so to Maggie's mother.

And what age would you like her to act? Maggie's mother wants to know. What should she be accomplishing at four?

Four! Mrs. Bailey is mortified. I thought she was at least eight!

Maggie is so tall and she will always be tall, her body rushing her to the size of an adult. And Maggie's always hurrying as if she's trying to meet that person she will become. She hurries to the tire swing. She hurries to the bus. She hurries to eat her dinner and her stepfather, the Psychologist, makes her eat every bite. Sometimes she gags. Sometimes Maggie's mother sits at the table and cries about this. Sometimes her mother grabs the plate and fights with him.

Maggie listens and hopes her side will win. Once she saw the Psychologist hitting her mother and ran between them. The Psychologist hit Maggie by accident and she flew from one side of the room to the other and it didn't hurt. The Psychologist was so shocked he left the house.

She doesn't think about fights. She rushes until it's time to go to bed and dream.

Maggie likes baths but only when her mother is the only one home. When the Psychologist is there he comes in to pee and accuses Maggie of trying to peek around the shower curtains. Maggie's heard the word repression. She knows that hers mustn't be broken or she'll have no conscience. The Psychologist likes to swat her wet butt because then it sounds the loudest.

Maggie tells Mrs. Bailey, We have a wooden paddle at home named Mr. P.

Mrs. Bailey wants to know how often it's used but Maggie starts talking about swimming instead.

She says, I love to swim in the lake with my granddad.

He comes to get me almost every weekend when it's warm. I like having almost no clothes on, the way the water feels rushing between my thighs and on my arms. The way it flaps against my stomach. I like to splash water high in the air, then swim down deep inside until it gets dark.

Oh my, says Mrs. Bailey.

Maggie listens to her mother talking to Mrs. Bailey, but she doesn't care. She is far away and nineteen. She lies beside a man. She is in Baltimore. She hears the neighbors arguing. In a Bronx accent that grates on Maggie's ears, a woman cries, "Harry! Harry! Harry! Did you get the crack?"

Maggie's mother frowns at Mrs. Bailey. She is tired of people expecting too much of her daughter. She takes Maggie's hand and Maggie smells the perfume she loves. Once she had a teacher who wore that scent and all day she felt like she was with her mother.

She runs ahead. They are walking home today in the bright New Mexico sun in spring. Maggie runs too far ahead and her mother is calling. She turns quickly and finds her mother there, still coming up behind.

They stop in a playground. They swing with Maggie in her mother's arms, happy to not be home. For so long she just sits there being swung, listening to the air rush back and forth until her mother asks, would you like to slide?

Maggie doesn't answer. She is with the man. He grabs her hair. He kisses her until her lips feel bruised. He runs his lips over her neck.

She goes to the store with her mother. She loves Cocoa Pebbles and her mother buys them and Skittles and brownie mix. So much sweet pleasure! Still, Maggie fears it will run out too fast. She runs up and down the aisles, hurrying and looking but not asking. Each trip to the grocery she's only allowed one request.

Her mother sits her inside the basket to help her keep still.

At home Maggie reads. She reads all the time. She tells her mother she wants to marry Jughead when she grows up. She tells her mother about Raggedy Ann:

You know why this book is so good? Because it's like you are right there with her.

She reads in a magazine about a boy who was stolen and found. One day she will feel there is no difference between the two, but now she wishes to be stolen and found.

Mama! Mama! If I were stolen, what would you do?

I'd search to the end of the world until I found you. Then she frowns and says, why do you ask me that? Her mother's fears are not secrets to Maggie. She likes to see them in her mother's eyes, for her.

Because I just don't know how you'd ever find me. Thieves plan carefully how to hide little girls and boys.

Maggie goes to her room and turns out the light. She is a bed-wetter and she lies on a plastic air mattress. The Psychologist punishes her when he finds the sheets wet. Through her window she can see the sky. Her daddy is a blue star she prays to.

She wakes crying at night. She used to be able to run to her mother. She runs to the door and waits there wishing her mother would hear her whispery movement and come to her. The Psychologist says little girls can't be getting into bed with their parents. She stops crying. She stops waiting.

The man is with Maggie in another room. He is old as her daddy would be if he were alive. He removes Maggie's sweaty t-shirt. He unbuttons her jeans. It is Easter. Easter has always been nice, coloring eggs with her mama. Lilies on the tables to plant later outside. Maggie likes it that the man has traveled the world playing in bands. He has loved many girls. He has four children somewhere. She wants to be a little girl with him. She's hurried to this place and arrived.

She hears the neighbor woman crying. She sits up in bed and looks out the window. The man and the woman next door stand on their porch. The man backhands the woman and blood spews from her nose and mouth, splattering on white walls and dirty windowpanes.

Maggie is wasted and she's run out of money. Maggie calls her mother and speaks to the answering machine. "I hate living in this part of town. My friend's in a porn mag. I'm drinking too much. The neighbors are white trash. Black men harass me on Baltimore Street. Talk about prejudice. You know they actually call this place Pig Town? Oh God," Maggie says. "Never mind. I love you." Her mother will be so upset when she hears that message, but Maggie can't take it back.

She is a little girl and her mother calls her to the kitchen in the morning. She loves the smell of vinegar and dye. With the wire holders her mother shows her how to stripe and dapple the eggs. Maggie's fingers turn pretty colors, then black.

Look at your beautiful eggs! her mother says.

Maggie arranges the dried eggs in a basket of lime green straw.

The kitchen is hot and Maggie has worked so hard she sweats. Her mother takes off Maggie's gown and opens the door and Maggie sits in her panties with wonderful air coming over her. Goosebumps travel her body. She doesn't want to eat but her mother makes toast anyway. She steps outside and scatters crumbs for the birds on the brick fence and on he ground and then on her stomach when she lies down. She watches the black birds hop her way. One comes right up beside her and she can see the bluish membrane covering and uncovering its eye. It pecks at her stomach and she reaches a finger out slowly, touching the blue shimmering in its feathers as it flies away.

Maggie and her lover are full of such longing. She is wise and knows it's time to stop wishing for what they wish for. He is so much older than she and waits for the wonder in her. He wants to feel it through her. She is a pale, pale girl and usually that paleness is beautiful. Now she is gray though her skin still perfect. Her eyes so large and blue now with the deepest shadows. She asks him to draw the window shades, to bring the bottle. She wishes to live with open windows. The neighborhood stinks. The fruit rots. Stray dogs dig in the trashcans.

The man jerks her hair gently. "Are you asleep? Am I that boring?" She longs for him to keep tugging on her hair.

He leaves the room.

She was asleep and now she's just tired. She drinks a beer. She goes to the bathroom and vomits. Her body is full of bruises. Bruises for no reason. Her arms are full of tiny punctures. She flushes. Her lover is coughing in the next room. She hears him through the wall.

She cleans her mouth. He comes back into the room. His eyes are so blank. She grabs his hair. She wants it to be longer. She wants it to hurt when she pulls.

Maggie! Sweetie! Her mother is calling. How did you run into that door?

I was just thinking, and you know how sometimes when you're thinking, you can't see?

There's a message on the machine. "Maggie, honey, do you want a ticket home?"

Maggie calls back, "I haven't eaten for days. I can't stop

crying. I feel like I have the flu, but it won't stop. I'm sorry for telling you about Susan. Anyway, she's not doing anything with anyone. She's just spreading her legs. I think I want to come home soon, but I'm not ready yet."

The man is impatient. He wants to go to a bar. They watch Susan dance on stage. They watch her take off her clothes. Maggie knows the man is aroused. So many girls have aroused him. She looks out the window at a sign sparkling with happy colors: yellow, orange, red and blue. On the wall above the window, false beer pours from a Bud Light sign. She looks all around the place. She loves the cheesy lava lamps. The man turns her face to his. He kisses her slowly. He touches her slowly, slower than the lights. She pushes him away. I want a drink, she says. He grabs her arms tightly so that she cannot move them. He looks her straight in the eye and she looks back. He laughs nervously and goes to order. Susan dances on the stage. She throws her panties at Maggie who throws them back.

A biker comes up in all his leather and chains. He has his hand inside his belt.

"I need a bourbon and seven," he says.

"Sorry," Maggie says.

"A bourbon and seven," the biker says. "Wild Turkey."

Maggie looks behind him at the bar in the distance, so far to walk, all those people making deals. An old-time register rings.

"Sorry," she says. "I'm not working tonight."

Maggie! Maggie! Her mother almost sings. What are you thinking? Are you hungry? Would you like to go to Peter Piper Pizza and play the games?

It is spring and Maggie is five. They live beside the college campus, beside the park. Maggie's mother is always reading, always studying for tests and she's married to a Psychologist. When she is not studying for tests she looks up at Maggie and she knows nothing.

Come on, come on, little desert girl. Maggie walks to the living room with her mother. There the Psychologist sits. He is an expert in children. When Maggie is alone with him he tells her of all the children's sorrows, of their broken bones, abandonments and scalding tubs.

Her mother braids Maggie's hair and wraps it on her head in pretty circles secured with butterfly barrettes. She presses Maggie's cheeks in her hands. Oh that face, she says.

She looks closer. What's wrong, Maggie? She gets a washcloth and wipes Maggie's face. She frowns at Maggie's arm. Always bruised, she says.

The Psychologist says, She's an easy bruiser and she plays too rough.

Maggie's bottom is hidden with all its bruises. Once the Psychologist gave her mother a black eye and said, You just want everyone to see and feel sorry for you.

Then he was sorry, sorry, sorry himself. He never gave her a black eye again.

Maggie will find a way for someone to see, a way he can't blame her for.

But then her mother is ill. She stays in bed for days. The Psychologist takes Maggie to the bedroom door to look at her mother lying there, but Maggie can't go in. He says she might catch what her mother has and die. He tells Maggie her mother is dying and when she does it'll be just the two of them. Doesn't she want it to be just the two of them? Doesn't she want to stay alive and not go with her mother? He asks her over and over until she says, yes. He sits with Maggie on the couch. He shows her pictures of her mother in various states of undress. Isn't her mother pretty, he asks? Isn't she sexy?

But Maggie's mother gets well and Maggie is so happy and she will find a way to make him leave.

Maggie is hundreds of miles away and congested. Now she is always ill. She sits on a couch in her living room in Baltimore beside the man. She is watching Susan tell stories.

Susan is twenty-four, Maggie tells the man. And all she's got is made up stories. She can't help herself for lying. She hasn't done a thing with her life. I don't want to end up that way. I want to do something with my life in the next five years. She feels the man's breath against her cheek, moist.

He takes her hand and they go out to find another bar.

Maggie's dancing is something to see. The way she feels it all. The way she has no inhibition.

They go sit down to have dinner. A woman is crying at a nearby table. Maggie turns off the overhead light and looks out at the stars.

"Look at me! Look at me," a man is saying to a woman at another table. "Don't you know all I've ever done, I've done for you?"

"Hey, asshole," Maggie says. "Hey! Fuck yourself. Don't you know that's never true of anyone?"

Maggie's mother touches her face. Maggie and her mother stare at the empty table. There is anger everywhere, but not in the Psychologist's eyes.

You'll still come see me, he says to Maggie. While I work it out with your mama and come back home to you.

Oh, I never want you to come back, her mother says. There's no question there.

Maggie wonders what she can do to make it certain she'll never have to see him again.

She waves from the doorway while her mother looks in the garden. The rosebush is high with fragrant roses. Together, mother and daughter cut some to take inside and they are free and her mother stays in bed a few days and doesn't get up, but then she is all right, just like before.

That is over and it's another time.

"You've been sleeping all day," the man says to Maggie. He is practicing very poorly on his guitar.

"Goddammit," Maggie says. "I'm so tired of rockabilly and now I'm tired of punk, too."

Everything is white—the sheets, the walls, the comforter. There's a hole in the wall and Maggie sticks her arm inside. She takes out a baggy of white powder. "Sorry, I lied," she says.

He looks disappointed and hungry.

"I think you're going to have to leave soon," she tells him. "Your problems are too old and I'm just a teenager trying to get my life started."

"Would you want to get married?" he asks.

Maggie laughs. "Oh, let us be married, too long we have tarried." Her flu, her crying are getting better.

She gives him the powder. She picks up handcuffs and cuffs him to the bed. She goes back and sits on a chair.

"Hey," he says.

"Not now."

"Then undo me."

"I'll undo you when I'm ready. I'm not joining you on this one. Don't you feel good yet?"

It seems like hours pass and she's sleeping and then realizes he's sleeping too, his arms out like he's crucified.

Outside the door her mother calls. Come on, Maggie. Sweet Angel! Come on and let me give you some medicine.

She watches the man drool. He is alive but he cannot cough. There is more. Maggie puts it back in the wall. She grabs a blanket and wraps it around her shoulders, twists ends tightly around her arms. She crawls under the bed, into coolness, hidden in dark, where she is relieved to feel no cobwebs. She wishes her mother were there to hold her. In the morning she will call. She runs fingers through her own hair. She reaches. A piece of lint bounces up and falls into her outstretched palm.

Carriage

The thread just keeps coming, bundles of aqua in her palm. She wonders how much damage she's done to the sweater's shoulder seam, gets up, smoothes the wrinkles from her skirt and begins the climb up the steps to the light switch, to the mirror. An alphabet block left by a grandchild almost trips her, so she watches her feet the rest of the way over the worn wood. She thinks of paths. She wishes for nimble fingers to fix her clothes, to knit the sweater back like it was. Standing on top of the stairs she hears the jingling of reins. The sight of a horse-drawn carriage takes her breath, so odd and beautiful over the snow outside. She leaves the light off. A tractor grumbles far out in the field. She dreams of running, finding her way back to her mama's house. There are paths still worn out there, beneath the snow, paths where she, a child, used to wander, dreaming, paths that lead to the front door no longer there.

Violin

He sat fiddling with the lace tablecloth, thinking, "*All done.*" Realizing this. Out loud, he said, "My gal." He'd confessed too much all at once with no time to sort and explain. Light shone on the crystal on the table and hanging above him. He thought of treasure. How silent it was now, the chair across from him, empty. He wondered about the price he'd pay, what the fee was for illegal parking.

Train

On the train there was a woman in pearls kissing a little dog that looked like a rat. Her skin was white as milk and her blouse very low cut. Her breasts rattling with the train and Coeli found herself thinking, milk shake milk shake milk shake along with the engine noise until music came over the intercom and she tried to remember the name of the tune.

It was from an album a friend had given her long ago, a friend who died way, way too young. It was Keith Jarrett's Koln Concert from the half of the album set that had been stolen along with her stereo, stolen by someone who probably never listened more than once or all the way through. Coeli remembered going into her bedroom and seeing the empty space where the stereo had been. She remembered the thin white curtains billowing away and against the open screen-less window in that old house in Mesilla.

She remembers not long before when her friend was still alive, she'd met an old man in the grocery who talked to her baby in the basket, who said, "Won't be long till she'll be old as me, seems like a long time, but it's not." She watches fields flying past outside as the train moves on. She waits for the wine to come round and holds onto that man's words like a lingering prayer. The milky woman already has wine. She raises her glass and says, "Cheers," and kisses that little dog again as he wriggles free from her hand and presses his paws against the sideboard to gaze through the window glass.

Zest

Into tiny pieces, she chops cucumbers, finally doing
something, making a salad, since her daughter has passed.
She will make the casserole with ham and potatoes,
something they all loved, something her daughter loved.
The family. She drops grapes over leaves. But when she is
making the dressing, grating the lemon zest, her hands stop
working, that word sounds so wrong: zest. On the counter
by the phone numbers people have left for her, by all the
flowers, she leaves everything unfinished. Later she will come
back. Her husband stands in the middle of the room by the
fireplace. He doesn't live here anymore but he did not knock.
Now he thinks there must be forgiveness. He loves her so
much. The buttoning sequence is off, the sequence of that
white wrinkled shirt. She undoes him. She can feel, she
knows how he wants to collapse right there with her. The
bed is too far. She considers the floor, but she cannot yet.
There is no going back. She wants to envy all the lovemaking
going on in the world. She wants that feeling of envy. She
desires the air, the feel of the glass over the paintings in the
room. There is dog fur in the corner. She takes a broom
and begins to sweep.

Sheets

There had been so much lightning. The power stayed on, but they didn't have a phone anyway. The girl wanted it to be just the noise that had scared the child, but the quiet brought no relief. The baby boy cried and cried, clawing at his flushed face in the dim night light while a ménage of toy animals twirled above in time to a lullaby. She paced in the hot kitchen, listening to the baby and the lullaby in the next room, the motorcycle revving in the yard. She didn't want to ride a motorcycle to the hospital, to carry her baby that way. Why didn't they have a car yet?

The motorcycle quieted, purring now. She could hear the frogs out in the swamp. The camera lay on the table with all those pictures they'd been taking earlier in the day, the dancing baby at her friend's knee. Now everyone was gone, miles off in Baton Rouge. She touched the child's cheek and it burned.

Her husband staggered in. Even feet away she could smell the whiskey.

They lived so far out and she didn't know how to drive the motorcycle, didn't trust him to hold the baby.

A light bulb snapped and turned the room black. She gathered toilet paper to cover her fingers while she twisted the bulb free. She rifled through drawers for a new one. She wished darkness would quiet the baby, but it did not.

She managed to find a new bulb and fumble until it was secure in the socket. The light came on and her husband stood there, in the same place. She didn't know what he'd been doing all that time in the dark, but strong as he was with those arms and those eyes, she could see his utter uselessness.

"Ready?" he asked.

Outside the rain started up again, sheet after sheet of it. She shook her head and dissolved aspirin onto a teaspoon to feed the baby. In a towel she collected ice and gathered the child into the cold cloth, waiting it out until morning.

Blue

My grandmother chopped the first snake I ever saw in half with a hoe. I wasn't afraid. Neither was she. Then I learned anyway it was only a king snake stealing the eggs. When I found out she died, I was sitting on a porch. I'd just left her bedside, made it down the road before the tornado tore over the hospice. A TV inside the house made the porch glow in flashing neon. Above was a blue moon. I couldn't get over how she died on that blue moon and how spooked her children were that the life had left her body and headed out with that tornado beneath that moon. How much sense it made to everyone. My dress felt cold against my skin. My mother-in-law was in the house behind me where I'd asked her to stay and leave me for a little while and let me just be sad. She kept telling me not to. She was so confusing. Her husband brought me a stiff drink and we laughed about being watched through the window in that neon glow. That last night of my grandmother's life, all the snakes hid in the woods. I watched the moon wishing to have time back and in awe that it was hanging up there blue.

Oysters

We argued in the kitchen. "I believe in pain," he said, and it made me mad.

"Stay away from me with that," I told him, and he went back to chopping.

"I hate onions," I said.

He grinned at me. "What you got against onions?"

We were stoned. We'd smoked with the boss after work. We were old enough to do what we wanted, but when his mother came out of the bathroom to leave, I was shocked to see her. She smiled. I'd waited on her that week, and when she kept talking about him and telling me he'd make anything she wanted, I asked her who she was and she said, "Epicurus," drunk and laughing and hoping to make me nervous.

He was shaping falafel and heating the oil. We were in his apartment, not in the kitchen at the restaurant. I watched his mother walk out the door, and told him, "I like your apartment."

He shrugged and looked around.

"Why?" he asked. "There's nothing here."

"The simplicity," I said, figuring it out.

He had started some drawing on the wall, from the

floor up. The straightest of lines turning in to something, all black and white, made it half way up.

The ceiling fan moaned above us.

We talked about New Mexico where I was from and where he wanted to be. He'd run away from Mississippi when he was a teenager and gone to New Mexico and dreamed of going back. He didn't know why he ever left except that he was so young.

He turned off the burner on the stove and wrapped plastic around the falafel balls. He said, "We should go get oysters instead."

"I thought you were a vegetarian."

He laughed sort of wickedly. "Oysters aren't sentient beings."

Outside the window, on Fortification Street, cars smashed together.

"That was a big bang," I said, and it tickled him so much. We did care, but we didn't have to call. The cops were already out there. The blue lights splashed over the streets and buildings, splashed over the walls inside the apartment. I looked at the drawing. Those perfect lines. I knew nothing of his talent except that he could make anything taste delicious. I'd see it later in the paintings around his closed coffin, black poor children rendered vivid with movement and brilliant color, with love. I'd stare while his mother wailed like I'd never heard such sadness before, and our boss, the one who gave him the drugs that meant don't call for help until everything is hidden, talked about cutting him down from that fan, about the life still being there for a little while. How it was too late to save him. How they looked each other in the eye.

The Sitter

M iss Marie came to sit with the dying. Before entering, she paused to marvel at lions and giraffes carved into wood. She didn't bother using the brass knocker. She stepped right in.

She'd never been in this house, but everything felt laid out for her convenience, like the doily on the bookcase by the entrance where she dropped her keys. Farther in she found more animals carved in wood. Hooks protruded from elephants, chimps and spider monkeys. She hung her purse here. Even close to the door, she didn't think she should worry. This wasn't a neighborhood you'd expect anyone to sneak in and filch anything.

"Hel-loo!" she called.

To her left was a box and a trash can on the floor by a piano. Someone had sifted through the contents inside the bench. A nurse startled her, sitting right there on a love seat eating a hamburger.

"What a mess," Miss Marie said.

"His daughter's going through everything," the nurse said, rising and smiling.

"Cain't she wait 'til he's gone?"

The smile disappeared and the nurse looked shocked. All the politeness drained right out of her face. She dropped her hamburger in the bag and crumbled it up. Miss Marie felt as if she'd turned invisible.

The nurse put a hand on her hip and stretched. "He's been talking in his sleep," she said to the air.

"I brought a Jane Goodall article," Miss Marie told her. "I checked around and found out what he's interested in. My research led me to discover he's contributed money to chimp sanctuaries. I thought he might be interested in new developments in the field. You never know what he might can hear."

"Some believe that," Nurse said. "I don't doubt it." She pointed down a long hallway. "His room is at the end."

Miss Marie headed that direction. Upon entering a large bedroom, she heard the front door open and close. The quiet ticked luxuriously. She felt alone and intimately close to the man in the bed, as though this had become their house, as if she had been invited home and was seeing it for the first time.

"Why, Mr. Lowe," she said, "your bedroom is as big as my house."

White satin swallowed the man up like a child, tubes and IV needles wounding his nostrils and arms. Nothing was in his throat. She sat her article beside marble red pandas on the fireplace mantel and kicked her shoes off. The cheetah-patterned rug felt cushy.

She pressed fingers against his forehead. "You sure like your animals," she said, looking up at her image reflected in the ceiling mirror. "My. Well," she added, imagining her young self reflected above.

"You're hot, my dear," she told him, and loosened the sheets so he could move should he want to. "This room is stifling. Someone trying to smother what's left of you?" She opened the doors and there glimmered a pristine pool. It looked as though someone had recently been swimming. A shirt crumpled across a chaise lounge. Someone's robe lay fallen on the tile. She felt spied on.

"I guess you heard them swimming," she said. "Let me go check if anyone's still here."

She walked the hallway, calling, "Hel-loo!" listening to the echo from the high ceilings until she was satisfied she had the house to herself. In the kitchen she filled a bucket with crushed ice. From the bathroom, she retrieved washcloths.

She placed everything on a tray by the bed. "You have a Jacuzzi, you stinker," she said. "I'd like a bath in that. Have to get my grandson to put me one in."

She could tell his fever was high. His breath came deep and long. His chest sunk and rose. She pressed cold cloth on his forehead. "Baby," she said, "let's get your fever down and I'll read you something."

She pressed ice to cracked lips and waited until he swallowed. "There," she said. "Let's wait a bit and then I'll give you more." His eyelids fluttered.

"A penny for your thoughts," she said.

Outside, construction began clanging on water lines along the street. The sound was suction, long sighs for breath, moaning and whining that sounded obscene and rude to Marie inside this house where one only ought to pay respect and offer comfort.

She retrieved her article. In a cloisonné bowl she found a single freshwater pearl. "This belong to your wife?" she asked. "Did you take some trip to the ocean and find it there? I bet they's a lovely story behind this pearl."

She watched him breathing. His lips moved to murmur. You could tell even now that he was once a handsome man. "I'd a liked to have known you sooner," she said. "I'd a liked to help you lose your religion."

She draped her legs over one arm of the leather chair she sat in to read. She said, "Hope you don't mind me getting comfortable since we're brought together in such intimate circumstance. I know you as well as anyone, Jim Lowe. Like my mama used to say, you can be married to someone and not know them. My husband passed fast, fell right down dead in the doorway coming in from work. I had no time for preparing. If you stay long enough around, I'll research what happened to your wife, so I know how you came to be without her now."

A bird flew in and out of a clock soundlessly signifying the hour.

"I'm going to enjoy reading," Miss Marie said. "I've always thought animal rights, people such as yourself, fanatics, but maybe I'll come around to your point of view. I do like the chance to learn now that my children are grown."

The noise outside ceased. Mr. Lowe stirred. She thought he mumbled, "Darling, are you here?"

"Shsh," she said. "Just rest and I'll read."

Legs

In a red corvette he drove up. I saw through the trailer window. With that limp and those long arms polio left him with, he stepped out and started walking toward the butane tanks and disappeared. When he knocked I watched my mama's hand on the knob, heard his voice sparkling its way inside. Water rushed in the sink. Slicked back blonde hair and laughter entered the doorway from a childhood dream. I ran to the hallway bedroom and he after, calling, "Aren't you gonna hug my neck? Come give me some sugar."

I'd crammed myself up against the wall on the top bunk. I watched him grin and kicked at his hands with my bare feet. We both grew still. I flew off and into his arms.

My little Beagle was at his heels barking, making the window glass rattle like laughter. I knew my uncle was by himself. I missed the little black-haired boy and its black-eyed mother with those lashes and those lips and that soft voice that used to belong to him. I missed them for my uncle as he smiled and electrified the room. I pressed my palm against his chest and felt it pounding.

I was a child but I listened. I knew he'd gone to Bakersfield, left Mississippi. I knew he'd sold cars, some of them stolen. He'd never had so much money. Then he went to prison.

He was out but he was going back even though we didn't know it then. "Look here," he said kneeling now beside me and opening a bag. Inside he had a fancy sparkling collar for my dog. He knew what I loved. He couldn't stop the hugging, the looking deep inside your eyes.

You get used to it, he told my brother later about going back. You get so you don't know how to be out in the world.

In Mississippi, there'd been a slaughterhouse. There'd been manure and grass and the smell was home. There'd been gladiolas that lined all the walls of the gym where they danced for the prom year after year so many kids in his family and the gladiolas were ones his mother grew. He cut those stems from the garden himself. There'd been catfish to fillet, a father he never could please and never enough money to change your life.

Soful

Allison waits alone by the phone with her coonhound mutt, Soful, named for a homeless storybook character who had soulful eyes. Her husband searches for a place to live in Oakland, all the way across the country, and he's having a hard time. He calls and says, "You had to keep that dog."

He found a wonderful apartment that accepted dogs up to fifty pounds. He made the mistake of admitting their dog weighed fifty-six. The landlord refused to bend. She tells him it doesn't matter. She will never leave Soful. No matter what.

In the night she hears cats screaming outside. It is not the sound of their painful mating, but something terrible happening. Inside, she and Soful remain safe.

In the morning she oversleeps and wakes to the dog barking. He did not come to lie beside her and wait for her to awaken. He keeps her to a routine in the morning, and now warns of a visitor's arrival. She walks down the spiral staircase in her robe at ten o'clock in the morning. Through the windows downstairs, she can see the mountains all green and round with trees.

The sound of the river and the scent of gardenias streams through the open windows.

Soful keeps barking and pounding his paws on the door. Through its window, she can see a man. She expects a computer repairman. "Sit," she says, but Soful will not. She falters with routine and with discipline. She grabs the dog by the collar and opens the door. She realizes her mistake. No computer repairman appears there to blemish the morning but another stranger. All at once she takes in the worn leather jacket and the knife hanging from his belt, the dirty hair and strangely wooden hands.

"Pardon me," she says, because the man talks low and the dog will not stop barking and wants free of her hold.

The stranger does not raise his voice but he keeps asking for something she cannot make out.

"Maybe next door," she says.

In the monotone of his voice and the way he pinches one eye and glares with the other, she gathers a warning to quiet that dog. She sees the word, "dog," form on his lips. The word, "quiet." He steps toward her and she pushes the door, releases Soful who slams his paws against the glass and bares his teeth. She turns the lock.

His eyes are the eyes of someone who has done terrible things and long ago lost remorse.

The man stands on the porch for a while and then makes his way down the gravel road where she sees now the motorcycle she never heard. He stands for a long time holding his helmet staring at the neighbor's house and glancing back, deciding. The emptiness of the neighbor's drive tells her the family must be gone to church.

Finally the stranger rides away. She sits with a glass of water and shakes. Ice clinks in the glass and her knee dances. She makes a wish about her marriage on a fallen eyelash she finds on her hand, wipes it on the robe, "On something blue so it will come twice as true," as her mother used to say. Through the window she sees Shasta daisies.

Minutes pass. She calms down. The dog comes and puts his face in her lap, looking up at her with those lined-brown eyes with so much beautiful light deep inside. He whines. Of course he has to go outside in the morning.

She opens the back door and he takes off like a bolt. She calls. She thinks he runs to the field with the busy road not far behind. At the edge, he stops running but barks and barks. She calls and calls and finally steps out.

"Come and get your leash," she says, but he refuses to budge. He keeps barking excitedly and baying and walking in circles. She fears the stranger sits out there with that knife. She breaks off a daisy and sits on the steps. Pulling petals one by one, she says, I'll go, I won't go, I'll go… waiting to calm her fears. Fed up, she marches toward Soful, ready to teach him to listen. He wags his tail and barks louder. There in the grass in the circle he makes cries an unweaned kitten. It hisses and charges Soful, then falls back.

"Kitty," she calls as the tiny thing draws back from her hand and hisses. Soful breaks out in that dog grin with that tongue hanging out. "Kitty," she says again, and it looks up hopeful.

Back on the steps she holds the purring kitten in one palm.

Soful keeps grinning and wagging his tail with his nose down, searching, out there taking care of the morning business. In a little while she will call and he will come running.

Cisco

I didn't know he'd followed me until I saw the fat, balding bus driver kicking my dog like he was something diseased and evil. In the classroom, I kept imagining the sparkle of his tags and how he yelped and cowered away, how no one had ever hurt him before, how he didn't know what he'd done wrong. I kept wishing I'd had a leash even though wishing was useless. The desert rolled by so long and school was a place you had to go, had to leave home for. Cisco waited miles away. The leash would have done no good. I couldn't have walked him home. I kept imagining writing a letter to someone to let them know about the cruelty I'd seen and I didn't remember ever seeing it before. I felt like a coward, crying and not going after Cisco. There were blankets at the foot of the bed where he'd sleep at night when I got home. After he brought our pajamas to us from where mama laid them out in the little hallway room in the trailer. After we dressed, he'd bite hold of the hem of our shirts and tug us toward bed to make us laugh and mind. "Bed Time!" That word turning to joy and fun. I'd mind him. I'd smooth out the blankets and feel the warmth of his body against my feet.

Oil

She looped an arm around the child who had began crying because of the onions but now wailed like his heart would break. She braced herself for what might be the matter, but he could not, or would not, explain. When she plopped on the floor before him, he said, "Your eyebrow looks mad." In the humid air she felt as if they were made of oil, shimmering and smearing out of sight. She wiggled her eyebrows up and down at the silly boy until he forgot himself and fell into her droopy arms laughing.

Conservation

Over the deck she flicked the broom at fallen leaves and watched a sweep of birds rise up as if they were in a groove together, she and those birds. A blast in the forest signified that the hunters were out again on benders. Drinking and shooting. Another year of falling out of deer stands, mistaking toilet paper. Tissue for a white tail. They were camouflage, bringing home dinner.

Honeymoon

The boy wore a powder blue tuxedo and he tap danced around the house in shiny shoes. He wiggled the long tail of his fancy suit. When a stranger, a soon-to-be-new relative took his picture, he hid in a corner, ducking and laughing, always to be captured happy like that. His father was getting married.

His father kissed the bride, and through the window the boy saw a bolt of lightning behind the bride and groom, way out beyond his daddy's semi in the desert, way out on top of the mountain. His mother lived somewhere beyond that distance. She'd left him with her mother, who left the boy beside the road and called his daddy, saying, "Come pick the little bastard up. I can't stand him. He's deranged from all his mother's drugs and whoring." He might have forgotten this except his daddy talked about it often. How horrible that grandmother was with her crucifix and prayer beads and statues in the house.

He watched the whole wedding, ducking and smiling. There was a yawning, the door open, a churr in the dark outside. Unlatching the screen, he snuck out, running to his good grandma's house across the way. Alone, he turned on the TV and popped popcorn perfectly in the microwave.

He wondered if anyone would miss him, if the bride and groom were already on the way to the honeymoon. What magic now might come into his life?

Powwow

At dawn on a day nearing Easter, Lily wanted to sneak around and see if her parents had bought any more presents, any candy or stuffed animals. Yesterday the family had gone down to Grants and done some shopping while Lily had waited in the car. She already knew her mother had bought a giant dictionary because she'd seen it in a cabinet above the couch. They'd been practicing words. Each morning they started with a new one. She stuck her head out the small trailer window to try and see if her father was already gone to work. What she saw instead of her father was a Jemez man running barefoot. It filled her with longing to follow, his swift, silent movement, his long hair trailing after, the way he headed up the side of the golden red mountain toward the cliffs. Heights made her freeze with fear. She wished to live here long enough that she would know many trails and could work on losing that fear. She wished to live here always. She stepped out her door and into the kitchen. There would be no sneaking around. Her mother sat there drinking coffee. In the center of the table sat a basket of Easter lilies. "Speculate," her mother said. Her mother speculated about whether or not they should plant them outside in honor of Lily, to leave something behind that was her name. Would they grow in the mountains? They would never know if the flowers came up the next year and bloomed or not. They were always moving. Any day now, Lily's father would hitch the trailer to the pickup and off they would go, again."Speculate, speculate," Lily muttered. She went and turned the TV on with the volume all the way down. Her baby brothers were sleeping on the couch. On the screen a woman sang high and whispery as a mouse. Then pageant girls were doing cartwheels and twirling batons.

"Did the singing wake you last night?" Lily's mother asked.

"Yes, but it was interesting."

Heyya, yahna, heyya, yahna, started running through Lily's head.

"Were they having a pow-wow?" Lily asked, mainly because she liked the way that sounded.

"Some ceremony or the other," her mother said.

There wasn't room to do a cartwheel so Lily braced against the wall and stood on her head. She watched an upside-down woman wearing a tiara. She didn't know how in the world, but this woke one of the babies up.

"You're hyper," her mother said. "Why don't you take your brother and go to the store. You can buy some gum."

Outside, Lily scanned the cliffs looking for runners. She'd seen a funny thing once while riding in a car and she thought of it now. A convertible coming fast around a curve, the side of the mountain plunging on the other side of her, and the driver flew out still holding the wheel, and then back in. "Did you see that?" everyone kept saying. Her mother said, "His eyes were as big as silver dollars."

"Silver dollars, sand dollars," she said now. She walked along the arroyo, carrying her baby brother on her hip. The thin crust of dry earth crunched beneath her feet and turned to the softest powder. She felt it between her toes, wishing she was feeling home. She let the baby down so he could feel it too.

Open House

JD was worried. He knew his life was about to change, but he didn't know if it was going to get better or worse. Last night his daddy, who did not live in the trailer with Mom, Uncle Robert and Grandpa, came by as he did most every night. It was not unusual that his daddy stood by the door ready to leave at any moment with a beer can in his hand. It was not unusual that his daddy was mad about something. Most often he was mad at some idiot who didn't know anything about driving trucks, and sometimes he would get mad at JD and say to Mom or Grandpa, "Give me a couple of days with him. I'll straighten him out."

When he would say something like this about JD, Uncle Robert, who might be cutting hotmix off his boots with a knife or sharing a bag of chips with JD, would usually say, "You can't even straighten your own ass out. Leave JD alone."

And Mom would say to Uncle Robert, "Hush, don't get him started."

JD's daddy said, "She expects to saunter into town after four years and see him." JD knew who him was. His daddy held the beer can above his head and showed them how she might saunter by wiggling his bottom as he walked across the living room floor.

Mom said, "She is his mother."

"She's a fucking bitch," JD's daddy said. "A fucking slut."

Mom clamped JD's head between her hands. "Don't say those things in front of the boy," she said. JD squirmed, his cheeks wrinkling up underneath his eyes until he got his ears free.

"It pisses me off," his daddy said, fisting his free hand and punching through the air. "She's probably fucked everybody in Indiana." He motioned with the beer can in a way that made JD look behind himself, as if Indiana and all the horrible things there were in the fireplace and on the walls for them all to see.

"Now she's come back to finish up New Mexico."

"Enough of that filthy talk in my house or I'll throw your drunk ass out in the desert," Grandpa said.

Mom said, "Robert, take the child to bed. Get him out of here."

She squeezed JD into her arms, then covered his ears again, this time pressing softly. "Poor baby," she said. "You go on to bed with your Uncle Robert, all right now?"

"Not yet," he said.

"Yes, yet," she said, pushing him from her lap onto the couch next to Uncle Robert. It was an easy shove but he found himself caught between couch pillows with his feet up in the air. She said "Go on now."

"How am I supposed to feel?" Daddy was asking as Uncle Robert lifted JD into the air. "What if she decides to take him?"

"What would she want with him now? She can't care for no child," Grandpa said.

"Mom!" JD called as he was being carried into the hallway. "I'm not sleepy. Mom!"

"She's not your mom," Daddy said when Uncle Robert passed close to him. He stuck his face out next to JD's and his eyes were bloody looking and ugly. "She's your grandma." JD pushed his daddy's mouth away. The blond whiskers scratched his palm and got beer foam on his fingertips. "You're mean," JD said, taller than his daddy and braver, too, in Uncle Robert's arms. His daddy lifted an elbow as if he would smack JD with it but Uncle Robert said, "Ah, shut up, Wuss," and swooped JD from the room. The last things JD saw and heard were Mom covering her own ears and saying, "Hush, just hush, you're going to upset him."

And his daddy's reply, "Well, he should be told. He'll know the truth soon enough."

At the doorway to their bedroom, Uncle Robert swung JD high in the air, then flung him onto a cot.

"Asshole, dude," JD said, and Uncle Robert laughed and clutched his stomach in a way that made JD giggle too. Uncle Robert messed JD's hair up and knocked him over. "Ignore your daddy," he said. "Get some sleep."

With his foot readied to kick Uncle Robert should he try to tickle him, JD asked, "My mama's coming to see me?"

Uncle Robert asked, "You remember your mama?"

"Not really," JD said, and he did not, though he had heard about her from time to time. "Is she coming to get me?" He righted himself and finger-combed his hair.

"She's coming to see you. You're one lucky dude. Got a surprise mama coming to visit."

Uncle Robert had been heading out of the room, but he slapped the wall and came back inside. From high above his own bed, he pulled down a box. "Look what I have," he said. The box was filled with pencils. "Get your sharpener."

Even though Uncle Robert finished school just as JD began, he still kept a lot of books and paper in the room. He had even fixed up a shelf for JD at the end of his cot. From there, JD found his sharpener and handed it to Uncle Robert, who sat down next to him and began working on a pencil. The bed caved in some so JD was leaning against his uncle when he asked him to look closer at the pencil. On its wood was a tiny dump truck and the words Uncle Robert read to him, Rials and Sons Trucking. "See?" Uncle Robert tested. "Our last name."

Uncle Robert counted out six pencils and put them in JD's backpack, hung it on the door, flicked off the light and said, "Later."

Whatever else would happen, the next morning certainly started out wrong. JD woke up too late to say goodbye to Uncle Robert before Uncle Robert had to run off to work. When Mom was scrubbing his hands, he had wanted to ask her about what he had heard the night before, but when he got ready to, she screwed up her face at him and asked, "How do you tear up all your clothes?" It turned out there was a rip on his T-shirt's shoulder and Mom had no time to fix it before the kindergarten bus arrived. JD headed for the bus stop torn between being happy or sad. He twisted the thread on his shoulder until the hole in his shirt was big enough that even he could see it when he twisted his head around. He pushed his sleeve up and pulled the backpack strap over to hide it as good as possible. He was feeling sick, the cold made his nose burn all the way down his throat and his stomach growled so much he thought everyone would hear. The taste of soap was in his mouth from when Mom washed his face and he wished he'd eaten more cereal.

The bus pulled up. As the doors whooshed open, JD turned back to look at the double wide he had moved into only two weeks before he started school. Beside it was a smaller trailer he had lived in before then. In that trailer, too, he lived with Mom, Grandpa and Uncle Robert. He did not remember ever living with his mama, but he did recall the magic of seeing two halves of a home become one. He whispered, "Bye, Mom. Bye double wide," liking the feel of the words upon his lips so much he repeated them.

Inside the bus, he found a seat near the back. With his forehead against the window he whispered low and close to the glass. The sound stayed in his mouth. The breath pushed back against his lips: "My mama's not a slut. My mama's not a slut. My daddy is…"

When he entered the school building the quivering in his stomach bothered him less. He knew a tray with crackers and cartons of milk would be wheeled in before too long and they started out the day singing, "Do Your Ears Hang Low?" and "The Alphabet." In school he was not JD but John David and he had learned to write his name.

The teacher wore wire-rimmed glasses and was not so tall or old as Mom and she smiled all the time unless you did something mean like stealing or didn't pay attention. Then she would look at a kid so awful no one in class would cough or move their feet.

Everyone had behaved nicely for Mrs. Holcomb for days now because something very special called Open House was going to happen. The walls were getting fuller and fuller. Each child had an area where his or her work was displayed and there were even drawings outside in the hall. JD had volunteered to bring cookies to Open House, which had pleased Mrs. Holcomb very much.

In the back of the room were round tables where four children could sit together and do art. After reading them the morning story, Mrs. Holcomb instructed the class to go to their cubbies and take out scissors, construction paper, crayons, and paste. Then they were to sit at the art center.

John David hurried to get his supplies from his cubby. Hiding at the entrance to the cubby closet, he watched to see where Ruthie Robletto would sit. He came out and placed his supplies at the same table as hers and sat down.

Ruthie had shiny black hair and from his desk one day he had noticed there was blue in it. She wore braids some days. Other days, like today, the sides were pulled away from her face so that you could see real well the freckles on her cheeks and the tip of her nose. All down her back were ringlets. Always, she had a ribbon in her hair that matched a color in whatever ruffled, flowery dress she was wearing that day. Today it was banana colored.

On the board Mrs. Holcomb showed them how to trace their hands on the paper and turn the outline into a turkey. They crayoned the feathers many different colors and made a red dangly thing that hung from each turkey's neck.

Mrs. Holcomb circled the desks, talking about pilgrims and Indians and giant dinners. She was passing out eyes that had a movable black circle inside like you might find on a stuffed animal. You could glue these on your turkeys.

John David had finished outlining his hand and had crayoned in two fingers that became feathers when Ruthie said to him, "Let me see." She leaned close enough he could smell how clean she was, and when she scooted his paper closer to herself, he saw that her nails were painted pink. He wanted badly to touch her fingers. She pointed at his turkey. "You're doing it wrong," she said. "You're going outside the lines."

"No, I'm not," he said. He took his paper back. "You are." On the thumb he drew a smile.

"I don't like how you color," Ruthie said. He stopped with the crayon in his hand. His fingers were much fatter than Ruthie's and Mom had not gotten all the dirt out from underneath his nails. He scratched at some blue that had gone over the line, but Mrs. Holcomb walked by and said, "Keep at it, John David. What a happy turkey! You're doing great!"

After they finished, they left their art on the shelves underneath the window while the paste finished drying. They danced in a circle and John David had Ruthie's hand in his. He put his right foot in and shook around like crazy. Everyone was giggling.

The snack lady came to the door and the children returned to their seats. They ate crackers and drank milk while Mrs. Holcomb passed out reminders that Open House was in four days. Then they rested their heads on the desks and waited for the bell to ring.

When it was time to go home, John David removed a pencil from his backpack in the closet. Ruthie was taking her windbreaker from its hook. He tapped her on the shoulder. "Look what I got," he said to her.

"A pencil," she said, wrinkling up her nose.

"Yeah," John David said. "Look, see? They got trucks on 'em. And right there, see? It says Rials. My last name."

"I can read," Ruthie said, missing the sleeve of her jacket with her pretty hand.

"Want one?" John David asked.

She'd gotten her jacket on and used the pencil he handed her to tug curls loose from the collar. When she zipped up, a string of bears ran all around her stomach. "Thanks," she said.

"Look at it," John David said. "See the truck?"

"Do all your pencils have trucks?" she asked.

"Yeah."

When she turned the pencil between her fingers, he noticed that not only were her nails painted but on one hand they had stickers of balloons and flowers on them. "Where'd you get those things?" he asked.

She splayed her fingers out to look. "My mama gave them to me."

"They sure are pretty," he said. "Did she get them at Wal-Mart?"

"I don't know," Ruthie said. "What do you care? They're for girls."

"I wouldn't put them on my fingers," he said. "Stupid."

Ruthie put her face close enough to his that he could see a space between her teeth when she said, "I'm not stupid."

"Then don't act like it."

She had a pretty bag that she carried all her school supplies in. She picked it up and stuck the pencil inside. John David told her, "If you need another one sometime, just holler. I got bunches of 'em."

"Thank you," Ruthie said and hurried away without paying attention to John David's, "You're welcome."

Outside, John David stood by a fountain that had water flowing from the wings of an angel. From there, he watched Ruthie run toward the street. A woman with puffy, stiff hair stood on the sidewalk and hugged Ruthie before taking her hand and walking in high heels toward the parking lot. If his daddy saw Ruthie's mom, John David knew he would whistle and say, "Baby!" John David swished a hand in the water, then smeared it down his forehead, nose and chin. He closed his eyes and wondered would his own mama be so fancy and this wondering set off a daydreaming that lasted for days. He could picture her looking at his turkey on the wall, at his drawings of certain letters of the alphabet, at his pasted together pilgrims and outline of his own face. "What a fine job!" he could hear his mama say. Though he could not quite see what she would look like, he imagined her smell—clean like Ruthie's.

Off the bus, walking the gravel road to his house, JD saw that all three dump trucks were home for lunch. On the steps he removed his high tops and shook the dirt from inside. "Whew, I'm tired!" he said, stretching his belly out like Uncle Robert would, as he carried his shoes through the doorway. "What a morning!" He did a pretend yawn that made a popping sound in his ears and surprised him.

He was trying to make the sound again, when Mom said, "Put your shoes back on. You're going to work with your daddy."

"Why?" JD asked, but from out back his daddy was calling and Mom said, "Hurry up, now. He's waiting."

Mom handed him a sack lunch and slid the glass doors open but there were no steps there. "Jump," his daddy said. "I'll catch you."

"No way, dude," JD said.

"JD, come on. It's not far."

Jumping into his daddy's arms was like jumping into a tree, there were so many scratchy parts to avoid—sunglasses, the jacket zipper, the bill of his cap. His daddy's arms and chest were hard and skinny, not soft and large like Mom or Uncle Robert.

In the truck, they were up so high he couldn't touch Mom or Grandpa when he stuck his arm out the window to wave.

His daddy told him to roll the glass up. They were going to talk. He knew finally he was going to hear about his mama coming. There were so many numbers and letters and circles in the truck and all the cars down below them looked so small that JD felt like a giant ruler over a bunch of toy people. He pretended a gas pedal was pressed under his right foot, a gearshift in one hand, a steering wheel in the other. "Vroom," he said, clutching and accelerating along with Daddy.

His daddy was telling him: "This highway goes to Tularosa where your other grandpa lives."

They passed a car. JD shifted and grinned at the woman who was driving down below them. He could not see her legs or anything other than a dress. "Are we going to his house?" JD asked.

"No, we're going to turn off to Ruidoso."

JD pressed as hard as his foot would, straight through the empty air. The truck wasn't picking up any speed. His daddy was different when he didn't have a beer. He didn't talk like he was mad at anyone and he wore sunglasses, sometimes even inside the house. Grandpa had said this irritated the shit out of him. He had said, "I'm not talking to you if I can't see your eyes."

"Your mama's going to be in Tularosa in a couple of days. She wants to see you."

JD rested his head against the window. The truck shook him. Its roar tickled inside his ear and mouth. "My mama?" He tried not to appear too interested because he didn't want to get his daddy started.

"Yeah, your mama. On Thursday. That okay with you?"

"I guess," JD replied. He wasn't used to his daddy asking if something was all right with him. It was then that he decided the change the coming of his mama brought was going to be for the better. He rested his gearshift hand, simply steered. His daddy's sunglasses were aimed at him. JD could see his distorted reflection in their mirrors. When he leaned towards his daddy, his nose appeared gigantic. He sat back, his reflection more normal, and picked at the loose thread on his shoulder.

"Your mama and me never got along, but she loved you."

JD wondered who *could* get along with his daddy. The truck was having a rough time, climbing and curving up the mountain. JD kept the pressure in his foot so hard his ankle started to ache. He was afraid they would roll backwards. "Don't you worry," his daddy said. "All she wants is to see you."

That evening when they pulled up to the double wide, JD looked again at the smaller trailer beside it. These were the two places he remembered living in but now his daddy had confirmed that once there was another place and another mom. The woman he called Mom stood in the doorway waving at him. How had it happened that he had settled in to calling her Mom and not Grandma? He recalled clearly a time when she had spanked him for pouring laundry detergent into the dog's bowl. He had thought she's not my mom, not my mom, not my mom and imagined a terrible witch had stolen his real mom and replaced her with this one. Now he had been told about Indiana. He knew the truth.

"Grandma," he said, touching Mom's face. He made himself say "Grandma," practicing for Thursday. She held him on the couch and they watched *The Flintstone's* together. She told him it didn't matter what he called her. She was still the same. She was his, whatever he called her. Reflections from the lamp and TV sparkled on the walls and table tops as if the room were lit up by Christmas lights.

The coming of his mama made him very special, so special that in the next three days he grew tired of Grandma holding him all the time, pinching him when she picked him up, over and over again, giving him ice cream that had begun to make his stomach ache, and he couldn't breathe when she pressed him into her breasts. He also discovered that he could get away with anything. He forgot to close the door behind him, he asked for and received gum at the grocery store, and he stayed up later at night.

Every day he took a present to Ruthie, pieces of gum on Tuesday, pretty rocks on Wednesday. When he'd give her these things, they'd talk and he started telling her stories about his mama. He told her his mama lived far away in Indiana where she had important things to do. She had heard about Open House and wanted to see John David's schoolwork. Even though she was coming just for a visit, she might end up staying. They had an extra house for her.

On Wednesday, Ruthie said, "Divorced. Are your parents divorced?"

"Ruthie!" John David said. "What an awful thing to say!"

But when he asked Grandma after school, he found out it was true.

Thursday took so long to get there that JD was leaning toward not believing his mama would really come. But after school that day Grandma gave him an extra bath and dressed him in new clothes. The shirt buttoned up the front instead of pulling over his head and had a scratchy stiff collar that crept over his face. His new shoes were shiny black and they hurt his feet. He wanted his high tops back. He did like what Uncle Robert called his "new do." His hair, which had been shaven to near stubble, felt soft and tingly underneath his palm. Grandma made him sit on the couch and watch for his mama's car. The wait, with JD unable to play or eat because he might get dirty, felt endless. The fireplace made the room hot. JD just wanted to take his clothes off and have a nap. Grandma hurried to the door or window whenever she heard a sound. Living near the highway as they did meant JD got nervous over and over again listening to the cars pass, until it was finally real, finally his mama knocking on the door.

He did not know what he expected, since by the time she arrived he had expected so many different things, but he knew his mama wasn't it. She wasn't anyone he recognized. Her hair wasn't long or black, it was scraggly and cardboard colored. She stood in the doorway doing nothing except staring at him until Grandma hugged her. They smacked kisses and squeezed each other, saying things like, It's been so long, No hard feelings, Just look at him,

Isn't he a cute little thing, before his mama finally knelt and said, "Oh, come here!"

He was shaking, and as he walked over to her he felt like his arms and legs had fallen asleep. He was afraid she might think this jerky walk was his normal one. She hugged him as if she was afraid to touch him, no squeeze, just hands on his shoulders and a cheek against his. Her voice tickled his ear. She asked, "Are you ready to go?"

JD felt his face doing all sorts of crazy things, smiling and frowning without his wanting it to, and he felt like his eyebrow lifted up to the top of his head and he couldn't get it down. He answered, "No."

"Now don't be that way, JD," Grandma said. "Go on and have lunch with your mama. You've been looking forward to this all week." She nudged him. "Go on."

His mama had driven up in a shiny red car. Once she and JD got in, she reached across him and locked his door. When she cranked the engine the seatbelt zoomed up and scared him. JD waved goodbye to Grandma, who stood on the steps and held onto the screen as if she was holding herself back from running after them. At the end of the gravel drive his mama stopped the car. Tears were all over her face. "JD," she said. "John David." She put cool damp fingertips against his cheek. "I didn't picture you so big." She took his hand and said, "Look at your stubby fingers." His mama didn't have painted nails, they were shorter than his and ragged looking. She chewed on them. "My goodness, why'd they whack off all your hair?"

JD rubbed his hand over the top of his head, feeling the hair bristle beneath his palm. "I've already ordered a pizza," she said. "All we have to do is walk right in and eat. Are you hungry?"

He wanted to say yes but the word stayed in his head. He nodded.

His mama pulled onto the highway and drove very slowly. "You know what today is, JD? Did anyone tell you? He thought, the day my mama comes to visit, but didn't say anything.

"It's my birthday," she said. "I'm twenty-two today. Seeing you is my best present ever."

His mama was one of the littlest grownups he'd met. She had a voice that sounded like a teakettle as it begins to whistle.

"Look at you," she said and patted his leg. "Just staring at me. You can talk you know? I don't bite. Please don't be scared of me." Her chin wrinkled up and JD thought she'd start bawling again.

He laughed. "I'm not," he whispered like a frog. He cleared his throat. "I'm not scared," he said in a more normal voice.

While they ate pizza, his mama told stories about what a silly baby he'd been. She said he had taken forever to start walking and used to smear food all over his face. He made sure that he cleaned himself with a napkin after each bite to get all the cheese and tomato sauce off. She told him it was her fault he took so long to walk because she carried him everywhere. She told him so many things—how he liked to look at himself in the mirror and comb his baldhead, how afraid of water he had been, and on and on—that he thought maybe he was beginning to remember, too. For certain he was beginning to like her all right.

They went from his being a baby to now. His mama determined all their likenesses. They both had brown eyes, little ears and he would probably be short like her.

She slid with him down the Peter Piper slide, gave him endless change for games. They won enough tickets to get a Koosh Ball. She asked him did he have a girlfriend and he told her about Ruthie Robletto. He had never told anyone about Ruthie. "I guess I like her all right," he said.

"I bet she's the prettiest girl in school."

"Yep," he said, watching his mama smile in a way that made his eyes feel big and his face tingle like his head did when he touched his new do.

Before they left the restaurant he told her about Open House, and she said she'd see what she could do about coming.

On the drive home, he sat close to her and held her hand. She recognized places they passed that JD had hardly noticed and could tell him what buildings used to be before he'd been born. Alfredo's had once been Taco Villa. The empty parking lot had once been the Backdoor, a fun place to dance.

They passed the building made of black boards with hubcaps stuck all over it that meant he was almost home. He asked her did that used to be anything else and she said, "Not that I recall," and they passed straight by the turnoff to the double wide.

"Oh, no!" he said. "Back there. You missed it!"

She squeezed his hand. "I know. Let's ride a little more before we say goodbye."

"Are we going to Tularosa?"

She turned on the radio. "Do you want to?" Underneath his mama's sunglasses, he saw tears. All at once, he didn't feel like being with her anymore. He didn't like the music either. "That's too far," he said. "I bet Uncle Robert's home. Did you see if his truck was there?"

She shook her head.

"I better get on home now in case Uncle Robert's back."

"You can see Uncle Robert any time," she said and pointed. "Look up, there's the Running Indian. Want to go inside?"

"No," he said. "I can't help it. I got to get home."

The tires squealed before they hit the dirt and made a dusty U-Turn toward home.

For a while they were quiet and he thought his mama was irritated with him, but she pulled him close and he rested his head in her lap. "I told you, you don't have to be scared of me," she said.

"I'm not," he said and lay there with her rubbing his cheek and head until they parked in front of the doublewide.

He wanted her to walk inside to the room he shared with Uncle Robert and see his toys and clothes, but she said she really couldn't. She asked him if he might want to visit her in Indiana someday. He said no. She said she had to leave in a couple of days but she would write to him. She started crying again, this time hiccupping cries and JD cried too. He wanted to go inside because he had to pee. His mama was saying, "I'm so sorry. Don't hate me."

"I need out," JD said.

"Oh, please don't ever hate me. You just don't know." She was crying when JD's daddy pulled up in his pick up, opened the passenger door and told JD to get inside the house. He said, "You haven't changed. Two hours turns to four."

JD tried to open the screen but it was locked. "Hurry!" he yelled, wondering where Grandma was. Behind him, his mama was wailing, "What have you told him about me?" and his daddy was shouting filthy words at her. The elastic on his pants was squishing his belly, filling it with sharp pain. JD rattled the screen, hard enough he thought the glass might break. Before Grandma opened the door, he had peed his pants.

He ran past her and stood behind the couch. Grandpa went and stood in the doorway with Grandma. He shouted at JD's parents, "Take it somewhere else!" As easy as that, they stopped fighting. His mama drove away and Daddy came inside. JD started shivering. He was wet and cold. Daddy said, "Come here." JD could not move, he was so ashamed, nor did he want to tell his daddy no.

"I said come here."

Daddy walked over to him and said to Grandma and Grandpa, "Look at him. He's scared to death." He pulled JD out into the open. "Goddamn," he said. "What did you do? Pee your britches?"

"Leave him alone," Grandma said.

Daddy said, "One day around her and..."

"I said stop."

Grandma took JD to the bathroom and put him in the tub. Each evening he bathed himself but tonight Grandma washed him. He looked at himself, the soap on his toes, his hand, his chest, each time Grandma did, because the way she watched the lather made JD want to wipe it off. "Poor guy," she said, but she did not look in his eyes. She helped him into his pajamas. By the time they finished, his daddy had gone.

Grandma said, "Go on to bed. We're going to town for parts for the truck. Your Uncle Robert will be outside. Get some sleep."

From his cot he heard the front door close; the trailer grew quiet, empty of people. Each time he closed his eyes the day played in his head like a movie he could smell. His mama's perfume when she held him and slid on the slide, his parents fighting in the dusty yard. It occurred to him that he hadn't reminded Grandma to pick up Open House cookies. He let go of the Koosh Ball. Its strange shape in the darkness began to scare him. He made himself grab hold and throw it from the room. He decided to go find Uncle Robert.

He stared out the large glass window in the dining room. He could see Uncle Robert standing on a fender with the Trouble Light hanging from the raised hood of his truck. His face kept disappearing behind the hood, then coming back into the light. His shadow smeared out giant across the desert ground. In the light his eyes were hollow and he glowed in a way that reminded JD of a monster or a skeleton. JD knew the only thing to do was to make himself stop looking and go get some sleep.

In the hallway he thought of new words: divorce, Indiana. He thought of a tiny woman with a whispery, high voice that he did not know if he would ever see again and of himself as a baby who combed his baldhead and smeared food all over his face. In those hands that might turn out to be like his mama's or his daddy's he picked up the Koosh Ball. He put it beneath the pillow. Tomorrow he would give it to Ruthie. The idea made him feel good. He went to sleep dreaming of ringlets of blue-black hair, of fingers stickered with balloons and flowers, and bears that ran around a little girl's stomach.

The Man From the Little Theater

There was a man from a little town talking about Shakespeare and performing and how you did it right. He was horribly obnoxious. He had an ugly voice from nowhere. Affecting an English accent, but damned if he didn't say, "You-ge" instead of "huge." He wanted everyone around to think he knew everything about Shakespeare and his contemporaries. He complained about distances to airports, about where to put the emphasis. He had a theater and affairs with stupid women, with very young girls who were maybe also stupid.

He wore cheap tennis shoes. He had nowhere to shop in his small town but he thought he was all that and everyone was watching him. Some were.

There was a sad woman with Ophelia-long black hair who watched him. She was intelligent but she was lonely. She thought he was something. She thought she knew and loved him.

Woman

He sees her standing in front of her father's store. She bends to pick a bag up, her arm moves gracefully. He watches her look back at the road, over where his car idles. He thinks she sees him, for a moment that she will run to him, but her movement continues in a half circle as she turns and steps toward and through the glass doorway. Even as she's out of sight, he holds the image of her and hates her with all the force he'd ever felt in loving her. It will stay with him—the parting of her lips, the bending and reaching, the turning, the slender body and how you couldn't tell yet there was a baby, his first son, inside her. He will never speak to her again, except to promise as she asks to never see his son, he will never see her again.

Years later when his other sons ask about her, whom he loved and married, he will only say, "She was a pretty woman."

Four-Hundred Miles

There was always a coffee cup right there in the cab of the truck. The highway arced on through the endless sky, up toward the mountains. He knew a shortcut. He got out to open the gate, then he drove through and got out again to close it with respect for whoever might govern this piece of ranch land. He kept the radio off, waiting for dawn and all those colors, that feeling of waking up with the earth, and the animals outside. Crows speckled out everywhere, on the fence posts and over the grass. No one traveled the road alongside him except a prong-horned antelope who flew through the open distance and out of sight. Behind him, toward home, his babies were sleeping. His wife didn't need to worry about the landlord. The coffee cup warmed his hands. The long road took him away over the mountain, to work for a week and then he'd do it all over again. Unless he looked closer and saw the flick of the tail, or golden blinking eyes, the mountain lions high on rocks tricked his eyes into seeing nothing.

Ramble

Lily is not in school today because it's the weekend.

The laundry is started and Lily needs to go put it in the dryer. She gets change and takes her baby brother by the hand. She wants her mother to see how well she takes care of him. His face is clean and his diaper changed. He has the prettiest curls Lily has ever seen, white and golden-yellow mixed. Lily's mother is pregnant with another baby and she spends the days sick in bed in the back of their eight-foot-wide trailer.

Outside she carries that pretty boy and stands at the fork in the road, one direction leads to the houses where people live for years, the other to the line of travel trailers that park alongside Lily's, coming and going. She looks around at the things she's come to love, her path to the river, the mountains, the picnic table where she gets together with other kids and makes plans. She and Cheryl Russom are going to see Cheryl's big sister where she works at The Bitty Barn, a place that smells like strawberry soap and incense. From Missy they have learned to pattern and sew their own halter-tops and to henna their hair. Mr. Russom's Peterbilt is parked behind their house. Even though the man can hardly hear a word and he smiles all the time, it's never as fun when he is home.

Vacationers come here and she often meets them in the laundry, but no one is there today. In the dingy white room, three empty seats are sandwiched between three dryers and three washers. She asks strangers about their lives and they answer happily. They think she's exotic living here, and she is never shy around the strangers. She keeps thinking of the right questions. They talk about the train ride along the Chama River. Lily has never been on the train, but she has a place beside that river where no one can find her and she just goes to think while the water rushes past.

Lily gets odd jobs talking to strangers. As she walks with her brother toward the Russom's, a woman washing laundry waves from a doorway. "Need anything today?" Lily calls.

"Not today, Lily." The woman smiles weakly. She is pale and gray. She tells Lily how she hopes for a new liver and Lily knows that she sees in that sad face that the woman doesn't believe it will ever happen. She tells Lily that her work ethic will take her far.

Lily walks on to the Russom house. "Hello!" she calls.

Mrs. Russom looks up beaming, sweeping the ground in front of her house. Mrs. Russom has lines on her face like a homeless woman who's been in the sun and drinking for far too long, but Mrs. Russom wears a hat and she does not drink as far as Lily knows. She has a house full of near-grown children and plants that cover every table and corner and wall of the house. Mrs. Russom has six children, one more than Lily's mother will have when the baby comes. There are stacks everywhere inside that house, clothes and papers and books. The couch is a cot and when Lily puts the baby on it, he falls asleep.

Cheryl enters the room with her brown wavy hair. It is the thickest of hair and Cheryl is the only one in her family with it. Missy has straight long hair and pretty Billie Rose has straight blonde. They are a family of opposites.

In the kitchen, they dip lettuce in mustard and talk. They remove plants from the chairs and scoot them around on the table to have room. This is Lily's favorite house she's ever been in. A bonsai tree sits in the center of the table.

"I like your mother's plants," she tells Cheryl.

"Our house used to be a house where movie stars stayed," Cheryl tells her. "Filming movies in Chama."

"Which ones?"

Cheryl's grows thoughtful, and says, "I don't know, but Rock Hudson used to live here."

Lily studies the boards of chipping paint. "Who else?" she asks.

Cheryl shrugs and asks, "Are you really moving?"

Lily shudders, the sour taste of mustard in her mouth. It moves all through her unpleasant now. "I don't think so," she says.

She goes home and asks and finds out it's true. They are going back to a place where she once lived where she had a friend who was much older who scrubbed the house so there was never a speck of dust and everyday made tea with a precise amount of saccharine pills that her mother would come in and taste, inspecting. The mother, who required the bitter tea, had bangs curled high and sprayed stiff and wore Western shirts like some woman from long ago on the Grand Ole Opry. That friend wanted to be a singer someday.

Lily's mother looks in her face. "Don't be sad," she said. "We're like gypsies. Think of it that way and don't cry."

Lily looks outside the open door at a breeze rustling the grass. She tries to feel the gypsy in her blood.

Her mother says, "You were born to ramble," rocking and rolling the baby on her knee for a joke. The smile on her mother's face grows smaller. She stares out the window and Lily thinks she imagines where they will be.

Lily takes her brother's hand, but her mother says, "Leave him."

She heads for the river and when she sits in the bushes by the rocks she's gathered where no one has ever found her, she realizes she likes to come here and be alone. This hasn't occurred to her before. Since she was four there has always been a baby boy sleeping with her in bed at night, and sometimes, during the luckiest of times, a dog at the foot of the bed.

Once Upon a Time on Bourbon Street

E vening. Fourteen-year-old Lizzie wakes by the Mississippi River. The water smells like gasoline, and beneath that, faintly of fish and mud. She is hidden behind steps that lead back into the Quarter. Her leather jacket warms her. She likes to show it off. On the back is a painting of a man, Bob, smoking a pipe that friends from home made for her, a young man and his wife who want to teach her things about living in the world without hard drugs. *Just smoke pot*, they keep saying. The diaper pin in her eyebrow itches. She opens her lunchbox, the one covered with all the photos of Bettie Paige, and finds her cigarettes gone. A steamboat whistles. The lights of a riverboat not so far away are like flickering white candles. Hardly audible comes the sound of a man singing: "Corina, Corina, girl, where you been so long?"

She feels turned inside out and exposed. She reminds herself she hasn't been gone long at all. Bob Dylan once traveled around hitchhiking. Her mother dreamed of doing the same but was too afraid. Lizzie is not afraid. It's silly to believe the world grows more and more dangerous. It's as dangerous as it ever was. The sky is a ceiling of stars, bluer black here as it should be. At home at night in Mississippi, the Jackson sky turns oddly purplish. Lizzie and her mother have wondered whether the color comes from pollution. Here the music colors the air with the sun descending.

It is as if she is falling. The sky has turned upside down and she is being sucked into a hole with lights swirling in it. She pulls her feet away from the river and grabs hold of the ground. Rock and glass hurt her palms but don't pierce the skin. For a moment, she feels sick with panic thinking something will happen to her mother. When she closes her eyes she sees her mother's face peaceful in sleep in that house on Fortification Street, the house with all the roses and the old shiny hardwood floors. Lizzie's room faces a side street with bay windows she can slip out of with her cat. The cat waits for rides with her and when the cars arrive she gets inside and he goes off down the alleyways. Right now he must be at the window watching for her to come on home, locked inside because her mother does not allow him out.

"I'm all right," Lizzie whispers like a prayer her mother and the cat might hear. "Don't worry. Just leave me alone." She's done it now. She's in New Orleans. She opens her eyes and the sky steadies. Her fear ebbs away.

As she sits up, bottles clatter. There are beer cans beside her and broken shiny glass, an emptied fifth of Jack Daniel's. Her neck is stiff from lying on rocks and grass. The handrails of the steps behind her throw knife shadows across the ground. Another riverboat creeps through the water and the extra light brings the sparkling glass and shadows to life, sets them in motion. She wants to smoke, go walking back into the lights, see the singers and musicians, meet more gutter punks.

Lying on the ground beside Lizzie is an acquaintance from school, Spider, a fragile-boned girl who lives in a bad neighborhood in Jackson, a girl who is a virgin. Even though Spider has run away many times, there is something too soft about her, Lizzie thinks. She is a girl who drinks until she falls asleep shaking. She is a girl who has been drinking with her stepfather since she was nine years old. They were in a group of people, Lizzie and this girl, when they got to New Orleans, and then they were walking the streets alone. "Spider," Lizzie says finally. "Wake up." She nudges the sleepy, pretty girl until she rises. The lights absorb and beam out from her dark eyes.

"Where is everyone?" Spider asks.

"We'll find them," Lizzie tells her.

Spider fumbles in her pocket and pulls out a pack of Camels.

"Hey," Lizzie says. "Where'd you get those?"

Spider shrugs.

"They're not yours," Lizzie says. "You were bumming mine all day."

"What's your point? A guy gave them to me instead of change when I was spanging." Lizzie has learned *spanging* is what you call bumming for change.

"You stole my fucking cigarettes."

"Said he was quitting."

"I was with you all day. I didn't see it happen. They're my kind, filter-less Camels."

"A lot of people smoke these."

"You suck."

"You want a cigarette, I'll give you a cigarette, but don't be accusing me of stealing."

Spider puts her hand in her pocket and Lizzie holds her breath wondering if Spider has a weapon, what all she has learned from her stepfather who has been in prison. Spider pulls out a lighter.

Lizzie says, "Just give me a cigarette. The whole pack is mine, but just share." She doesn't want to fight. She doesn't want Spider to leave. She doesn't know where Louie, the guy they rode to town with, went. The thunder sounds again and she thinks of how Louie made it out of Slidell after Katrina by floating on a door with his Pit Bull swimming ahead and pulling him by the leash. She wishes they had a dog.

"Here," Spider says. "But I'm offended, you should know."

"Right," Lizzie says, deciding she'll take back what's hers later.

She lights and inhales and feels such utter relief that she helps Spider brush debris from her sweater. They head toward the music.

Hooves clatter along the brick streets beside them. Wheels turn.

"Mister! Hey, Mister!" Spider yells to a driver in a flowing white tuxedo. "Can we ride in your carriage?"

"Got forty bucks?" he calls, bowing forward politely with a smile for the pretty girls. They are both so pretty in such different ways, Lizzie so long limbed beside this little girl. Lizzie knows how people love her lips and eyes. She has heard people call her sultry. She has been told more than once she has smoky good looks. The driver waves goodbye and rides off without waiting for an answer to the question about how much money they have.

"Rich bastards!" Spider yells. "Who can pay forty dollars for a carriage ride? Doesn't anybody give anything for free?"

Lizzie says, "There was a guy giving hits of acid away near Esplanade."

"Do you remember the way?"

"I can guess it," Lizzie says. "Follow me."

Someone whistles and the girls turn around and see Weasel, a man they met yesterday. He's dressed in black and wears a top hat over his multicolored hair. He tips it to them then leans against the wall of Preservation Hall and waits.

Kids on the street say Weasel lives in a nice squat with running water. She hopes he'll take them there later.

"Where you headed?" he asks. "Didn't I tell you I'd be back to the river to find you?"

"We forgot," Lizzie says.

He thumps her on the ear.

"Ouch!" she says giggling. "That stings."

He grabs her chin in his hand. "Listen," he says, squeezing her face softly and staring hard into her eyes. He touches the diaper pin in her eyebrow. Before she can stop him he has unfastened it and tore it from her skin and she is bleeding enough he hands her a handkerchief, and the pin. "Put it in your pocket," he says. "I don't like the way it looks." He shakes cigarettes out of a pack and offers the girls one. Spider takes one. Lizzie sneaks two, watching the corner of his shifty eye. She hides a cigarette behind her fingers. He flicks his lighter, holding it before him and waiting for them to light up. Once they have, he grabs Lizzie's wrist and turns her palm up. He takes the extra cigarette from her hand and sticks it behind her ear.

"Don't think I don't see everything," he says.

"Sorry," she says.

"Fuck you are," he says and makes to walk away but says, "I asked where you two were going?"

"Graveyard," Spider says.

Lizzie dabs the handkerchief to her brow. She says, "I want to collect stone rubbings. Do you know the way to an above ground cemetery?"

"I'll show you later," Weasel says. He walks on down Bourbon Street. "Come on!" he yells. "Let's go spanging and catch the trolley."

Tourists ignore them.

Weasel walks right up on people, like it's a threat and he won't step out of their way. Few of them give him change.

They meet a New Orleans kid with a Mohawk and a black widow tattooed on his head. Spider tells him, "You're all shiny and new."

It's the same thing she said about Lizzie's leather jacket when they took off from Jackson and now Lizzie feels insulted.

The kid's name is Mal. He wears Doc Martens with a hammer and sickle painted on. He and Spider walk arm in arm. He asks her how she got her name. Birds rise up and something washes cold down inside Lizzie's belly.

"I'm a weaver of webs," Spider says.

"What does that mean?"

"Stick around," she tells him.

Lizzie says, "It's because she's skinny and wiry as a muppet."

"That's not true," Spider says. "It has to do with stories and love."

He frowns and pulls Spider more tightly against him. He puts a tiny piece of paper in her mouth. He gives hits to Lizzie and Weasel too.

No one asks Weasel how he got his name. He sniffs and sidles through the streets.

Mal goes into a store and steals paper and pencils for stone rubbing and puts everything in Lizzie's Bettie Paige lunchbox. The four of them walk several blocks to the cemetery, saving their change for a ride back.

They've climbed over a fence. Lizzie is alone on a tomb. She watches Mal pull Spider deeper into the cemetery until they disappear. Weasel sits there, the lunchbox open between them. He taps his leg with a stick that looks like a cane. They wait. The last birds fly into the trees to sleep for the night as the sky grows darker. Finally they hear footsteps. Mal comes out whistling. Spider is adjusting her clothes and making tracers that she follows with her hand. "Come on," Weasel says to Mal. "I got something to show you."

Lizzie can see well enough by streetlight and there are votives all around, bouquets of flowers. Spider stops making tracers and hugs herself into some quiet place inside as if she is dreaming a sad dream. Earlier Lizzie felt Mary praying over them, in a place where the shadow of the robes of a statue bent into the street.

"The tombstones are art," Spider finally says. "These intricate designs. Nothing like this is done anymore." She has sheets of thin paper in a notebook, pencils. Lizzie holds a piece of paper. Spider rubs the pencil across and across, over dragons, fairies and unknown symbols they decide to research in the New Orleans Library.

Lizzie says, "I don't think Weasel liked Mal putting his arm around you and going off."

Spider says, "Jealousy's stupid. I'll never belong to anyone."

"I want to find Marie Laveau," says Lizzie. "I want to make a wish."

A man comes from the shadows, standing on the ground below them.

"Where *did* Weasel go?" Lizzie asks Spider but the man seems to think she's asking him and he shrugs. He has long scraggly hair and only one arm. Spider screams, then Lizzie screams. Then they laugh at their childishness with those screams echoing over and over the graves.

"Thought you were a ghost," Spider says, recovering.

"Very much alive," he says.

Lizzie can't quit being startled at his sudden odd presence. She tries to amend her rudeness the only way her mother has taught her, with honesty. "How'd you get hurt?"

"Iraq," he says.

Spider's shoe presses firmly on her fingers and Lizzie gets lost looking at the shoelaces, how they wind and don't match. "That sucks," Spider says.

"Fucking government," Lizzie says, embarrassed now that she must have looked at him so horrified. Maybe he's a harmless bum, standing there with his whiskey in a bag, but you can never tell. There is a mole on his face that makes her think of pictures of melanoma she's seen in magazines. She says, "The planet's too hot and the government fucks us over, one generation after the next."

"You trying to impress me with anti-government talk?" he asks.

"Of course not," Lizzie says. She giggles descending from the tombstone, then holds out a hand to help Spider down.

He says, "Thought you saw a ghost."

"You were a surprise."

"Know why the tombs are so high up and in concrete?"

"The water," Lizzie says. "And whole families are here together."

"Now you tell me the sense of taking all this trouble to preserve dead bodies."

"Respect?" Lizzie guesses.

"You can't just throw away somebody you loved," says Spider. "At least you shouldn't. Besides it has nothing to do with water. It's all about tradition."

"Shit," he says. "Has nothing to do with any of that. It's just a sick, mummification ritual."

Lizzie doesn't know what to say. Concrete tombs tower above her. Angel wings and Southern Gothic designs stand high, but still below sea level. Fragrant flowers and trees drop petals on the ground. An iron fence surrounds them. The man says, "There's a weird one back over there," motioning behind him.

Lizzie hears whistling she recognizes now to be Weasel and then there he is.

"What you doing, motherfucker?" he says to the vet.

"Leave my girls alone."

"Your girls," Lizzie repeats, giggling at the silly possessiveness, but she sort of likes it.

"Get out of here," Weasel says to the man. "Go on." And the man walks into the cemetery.

"That guy's a rapist," Weasel tells them.

"With one arm?" Spider says. "Lizzie'd punch his lights out."

"Don't be so stupid," Weasel says. He shakes his head. "The degree of some people's misconceptions." He kicks debris as he walks away. He is wearing hammer and sickle Doc Martens.

"Where is Mal?" Lizzie asks and she looks into his face and realizes he is so much older than she thought. All the dried out lines around his eyes speak of somewhere beyond thirty.

"He's gone home to mama."

Lizzie nudges Spider and points to the shoes on Weasel's feet.

"You didn't hurt him, did you?" Spider asks. "I liked him. I wanted him to stick around."

Weasel shakes his head. "You need to find us someone," he says to Lizzie. He motions and they follow to the Trolley Stop. They travel on down the track, past houses and brick streets. She doesn't know how she could ever find her way back to that tombstone where she has forgotten her lunch box, and even if she did, would it already be stolen? Lizzie is wishing to find Marie Laveau's tomb. She is imagining turning with Spider in circles three times and making wishes. Everything moves and breathes and she wants to feel happiness coming from Spider, have fun following Weasel, but Spider feels to her lost somewhere, and Weasel's face gets older every time she looks at it.

Leaves twirl into the streetcar and the air is growing cold.

"Bet I can tell you where you got those shoes," Lizzie calls to a handsome tourist in a seat in front of her.

He turns.

"Bet you five dollars I can tell you where you got them."

"Girl, what you doing betting on my shoes?"

"I can tell you for five dollars."

"Okay, tell me."

"On your feet."

He is blond, dressed in loose slacks, stylish, green eyed and delicate. Quick and with a smile, he takes a five out of his billfold, hands it over and says, "Won't argue." She wants to be proud but it was so easy.

Weasel and Spider come from the back of the trolley and sit beside Lizzie and lean forward. Weasel scans the guy like a flirt and says, "You're not going to let her get away with *that* con."

"I already knew it. Doesn't everyone?" He holds out his beautiful hand. "My name's Randy," he says.

They descend the steps and head across Canal, the street busy with voices and bright colors. Yellow, violet and green flash by and they are in the heart of The Quarter.

Randy asks, "Can I buy ya'll a beer?" Then he squints at Lizzie. "How old are you?"

"Actually eighteen," she lies, knowing her height will work magic for her like always. Maybe Marie Laveau has brought Randy to her. Maybe he will turn into someone else in a minute too. "But it doesn't make a difference on Bourbon Street."

"Or anywhere in New Orleans," Spider says, and it seems as though she will never stop that strange hugging herself and looking like part of her has gone away into sad dreams. "What you want to do? Card us? Or have some fun?"

Randy steps to a sidewalk stand and orders four beers, but Weasel says they all want Hurricanes and Randy obliges, buying a drink for each of them.

"Do all of you live here?"

"Weasel does," Lizzie says. "The rest of us are just passing through."

"No, I don't," says Weasel. "I'm just biding my time."

They walk the streets and Randy buys them all another. He asks Lizzie why she's there.

"My mom sends me to school with a bunch of imbeciles. I took a test once and tested out of twelfth grade. I don't need it."

Lizzie thinks she is revealing too much like a child. She just wants to be here. She's tired of the loneliness of her room at night with the cars washing by and the falling leaves. It's a house too filled with only women and she wishes she knew her father even though nothing is really that wrong, he's just been gone since she was little and never came back. She says, "Please, let's not talk about all that now. It's Mississippi. It's depressing."

He rests his hand on her shoulder, then squeezes. "Sure 'nough," he says.

Lizzie thinks Randy's beautiful and kind and she is in love. He takes them to dinner and is a Vegan like her. They sit on a balcony drinking water from sparkling glasses and watching a piano band play down below. He talks about art and living in a small town and coming to a city filled with music. He is twenty-two. He has come here alone. He is sure he will find a job. He's not worried about that. He's not worried about the rain.

He wants their stories and Lizzie just says this time that

she's searching, she doesn't know why she doesn't want to be at home, and Spider says her home is no place she can live, that if she stayed there any longer her stepfather would molest her. Weasel whistles his alarm, but doesn't say anything. Lizzie notices the weaving veins of his hands, how they snake beneath wrinkles. He suggests they get a fifth of bourbon. They head for a corner store and buy a bottle to share.

Randy is turning to Lizzie, smiling. He is turning to Lizzie, smiling and so happy and moving and Weasel takes the bourbon from her hand and smashes it against Randy's face and beats him over the head until Randy is bloody and not moving. Weasel takes all the money from his clothes and the shoes from his feet.

Spider's gone, but Lizzie hasn't moved. She asks Weasel, "Why?" in the dizzy, empty alleyway.

His top hat falls off and as he bends to pick it up, she cries, "He was giving you everything. You didn't *need* to do that."

Weasel screams, "Come on," and stops his run in a sort of dance, looking back at her. "Come on." He shakes his head and starts running again.

Lizzie takes her leather jacket off and covers Randy because he is shaking. She looks down at the cartoon figure, at Bob, smoking that pipe and looking back at her. Then she starts running, too, in the opposite direction. Not far until she vomits, thinking of Randy's broken beautiful face. She tells a man beckoning in a club doorway, "Send help. Some guy got beat and maybe killed in the alley."

Walking away she turns back and the man is still in the doorway. "Believe me," she says. "Go see for yourself or something."

Back by the Mississippi, it's early morning and the town smells like vomited alcohol and spoiled bananas. Spider slips beside Lizzie. Mal has come up with her. He has a black eye, brass knuckles and chains, and Spider says, "Look who got his shoes back." Lizzie sees the bright hammer and sickle, and standing behind Mal is the Iraq vet.

Mal says, "He helped."

There is a bloody scab in the center of Mal's forehead that makes Lizzie touch the scab above her own eye. Mal has more hits of acid for each of them.

The vet refuses, lights a joint instead and sits down. "Too many bad trips for me," he says. "I give up."

Paper dissolves on their tongues. Spider says she's been looking for Lizzie for hours, ever since they got separated. She hands Lizzie a cigarette. Lizzie watches the water. She begins to cry.

"Hush, hush," Mal whispers, sitting down next to her and pulling her into his coat, against the warmth of his T-shirt inside. "Me and my friend here fixed him good."

The vet's silence is like ice.

Spider interlocks their fingers, saying, "A storm is coming. I'm going to another town. I've got a ride tomorrow. Mal's coming. Want to go with us?"

Lizzie thinks of home, that room with her watching mother. She feels the world expanding, moving inside her. Someone is tap dancing in the distance. She says, "Yes, I'll come with you."

The vet says, "I know a place near Decatur Street where we can stay the night."

A breeze sets the sky in motion. Riverboat lights flicker and swirl out. In her mind pictures spin—of her worried, pacing mother, of glass exploding, of Randy and his blood on the street. She wants to be with people who have seen what she's seen. Spider squeezes her hand. Mal pulls Lizzie closer as if he might shelter her from the wind, saying, "Shush, shush. It's all right."

"I came here to watch you," Lizzie says to Spider. "And now you're watching out for me."

The water laps. A riverboat whistle blows and images of tombstones grow, then melt slowly into nothing.

SPECIAL THANKS FROM THE AUTHOR

Thanks to Sara for the kid poem and to Brian for finding the title in it that brought this all together. Thanks to Toni Nelson for the talk over champagne that inspired putting the collection together, and for all the time in her wonderful house in Las Cruces. Thanks to Dana Kroos for those fiction discussions during wine o'clock. Thanks to Boz for his suggestions and encouragement in Taos. Thanks to Becky Hagenston for the insight and cherished friendship.

Thank you Kevin McIlvoy for being there at the start and pushing me along this path. You're there with me every time I write. Thank you again aunt Sis for that first computer. Thank you Mary Robison for believing so much in my work. Thank you Frederick Barthelme for the same.

Once again my deepest gratitude to my fellow Hot Panthers in Kim's room, and to my friends in Pia's room, all of them clicks away thanks to Francis Ford Coppola giving us the Zoetrope Virtual Writing Studio. What a journey we've all been on together. A toast to all you fine writers and friends, in particular: Stephanie Anagnoson, Grant Bailie, Terry Bain, Randall Brown, Kim Chinquee, Myfanwy Collins, Avital Gad-Cykman, Kevin Dolgin, Pia Ehrhardt, Pamela Erens, Kathy Fish, David Gerard Fromm, Scott Garson, Alicia Gifford, Tiff Holland, Roy Kesey, Liesl Jobson, Sue Henderson, Lindsay Brandon Hunter, Jeff Landon, John Leary, Pasha Malla, Mary Miller, Mary McCluskey, Jim Nichols, Jennifer Pieroni, Jim Ruland, Gail Siegel, Seth Shafer, Utahna Faith Skaggs, Claudia Smith, Scottie Southwick, Carrie Hoffman Spell, Girija Tropp, John Warner, and Todd Zuniga. Still missing you, Bob Arter.

Thank you Catfish for traveling the country with me. Thank you Maggie.

Thank you Taos Summer Writers' Conference for that DH Lawrence Fellowship, for that affirmation and for a rockin' good time. Thank you Sharon Oard Warner. Thank you Carmela Starace for the ride halfway around the Enchanted Circle with you and Dorothy Allison, the drinks in that bar, and the good talk everywhere the three of us went in Taos.

DARLIN' NEAL was the 2011 winner of the DH Lawrence Fellowship from the Taos Summer Writers Conference, their highest honor. She is a recipient of the Mississippi Arts Commission Literary Arts Fellowship, a United Arts of Central Florida grant, the Henfield Prize, and the Frank Waters Fiction Fellowship. Her first collection, *Rattlesnakes & The Moon*, was nominated for numerous awards including The Story Prize and The Pen Faulkner Award. Her short stories and nonfiction have been nominated a dozen times for the Pushcart Prize. An assistant professor in the undergraduate and graduate Creative Writing programs at the University of Central Florida, she serves as faculty advisor for the award-winning undergraduate literary magazine *The Cypress Dome*, and for The Writers In The Sun Reading Series. She is Fiction Editor of *The Florida Review* and lives in Orlando and Vero Beach, Florida.

Cover artist **ASHLEY INGUANTA** is a Florida-based writer/ photographer. Her work has appeared in *Redivider*, *SmokeLong Quarterly*, and *Sweet: A Literary Confection*, among other journals. Ashley is also director of Maitland Poets & Writers, a program that promotes literary arts in Central Florida, and she is a staff editor at *SmokeLong Quarterly*. Last year, she earned an honorable mention in *Glimmer Train* for their Very Short Fiction award. Keep up to date with her publications and travels at ashleyinguanta.com.

www.ingramcontent.com/pod-product-compliance
Lightning Source LLC
Chambersburg PA
CBHW020646250626
47154CB00008B/2837